# SINS OF THE WRONGED

*By*

*Daniel Lorn*

# SINS OF THE WRONGED

Written by Daniel Lorn.

All rights reserved.

No part of this book may be reproduced or transmitted in any form or by any means, electronic or mechanical, including photocopying, recording or by any information storage and retrieval system, without written permission from the author, except for the inclusion of brief quotations in a review. For permission requests, write to the author at the email address below:

daniel.lorn@outlook.com

All of the characters in this book are fictitious, and any resemblance to actual persons, living or dead, is purely coincidental.

Copyright © July 2024 by Daniel Lorn
First Edition Printed 2024

*It matters in life, what we do to them,
in preparation for the realms
occupying their death...*

## PROLOGUE

*Two silhouettes loomed resolutely beneath the thrashing rain. Cojoined by little more than tightly clenched hands, they allowed the raindrops to wash away any echoes of reality, concealing it under a fizzing tapestry of white noise. They sat that way for a while, gaining strength from the beads of water that danced against their skin before joining the puddles encircling their bare feet. Behind them and through the patio doors bordering the scene on the balcony lay an empty bed stained not just with the memory of their physical entanglements as lovers, but with untold truths yet to be shared.*

*Carmilla understood herself to be Maria's first love and consequently had allowed the dam built around her dark memories to yield to floods of tears. But as those memories of past events merged with the rain, Maria tightened her grip on Carmilla, offering a beacon of warmth against the cold breath of the imminent storm. She had proven to be a welcome distraction from the demons Carmilla battled with whenever the darkness soaked up the light.*

*As the rain continued its aggressive onslaught on buildings, trees, and them, Carmilla momentarily became one with Nature. Her senses were intoxicated by its burrowing fingers and by Maria's calming presence. But the stains of her past would return after the storm, as always. And Carmilla had no appetite for sharing her burden with her innocent companion.*

*Not yet, anyway.*

*They would separate tomorrow, but Carmilla would allow herself the mercy of one final night together before retracting herself from this false actuality.*

*The hiss of rain carried out from the balcony, rising into the sky as a protective sheet of grey over the washed-out world below.*

*A world filled with unfathomable secrets.*

## CHAPTER ONE

Autumn's breath misted the air as a final act of defiance against the decaying summer warmth. Green hills rose towards ominous grey clouds, which gathered low in the sky underneath the silent threat of a pending storm.

Below the hanging mists that topped the high peaks bordering the valley, a single car murmured down a narrow road unimpeded by the dominant and oppressive tranquillity which had flooded the atmosphere. The road was flanked by flat stretches of unkept farmland, intermittently scattered with abandoned outhouses and the occasional gathering of pale brown and grey bushes. Ash Woodland trees loomed tall on forest edges of the surrounding hills, defiantly holding back the imminent shedding of leaves to be sacrificed upon the altar of Autumn's arrival. Each branch would, however, be reborn, stronger and more robust after the eventual discarding of its seasonal skin.

Although reluctant to suppress its tempest, Nature temporarily relapsed to grant the car passage through the elements along this isolated country road, which would lead its two occupants to their destination.

*

Neither of them had spoken a word since leaving the motorway several hours ago. There was nothing left to be said. The car rumbled over a bump on the road, and Maria changed gear, accidentally brushing Dom's knuckles. His reaction was to pull away from her awkward touch—a sensation that had once excited them both now seemed to linger on him as a stagnant, unwanted stain.

Maria swallowed hard and fought away the tears which threatened to spill from her tired eyes. Although Dom appeared fine to welcome this distance, deep inside, she knew that she would never stop loving him. But she couldn't go on like this, living like a prisoner to a relationship held together with no more than a web of good intentions. Not unless he was willing to try at least and forgive her. She caught herself in the rearview mirror, where a hollow shell of a woman was fixed on her. Dark rings under her eyes from stress and worry. Her short black hair, ordinarily full and vibrant, was pulled tight in a ponytail, draining any remnants of colour from her pallid complexion.

Before drawing her attention back to the road, she caught a glimpse of Dom. Even at fifteen years her senior, he didn't display tiredness from stress or worry. Nor did his demeanour offer any reflection of her anxieties. He was a picture of health and contentment, with spiky hair complementing his lightly tanned skin and his fresh citrus aftershave concealing any scent of alcohol from the previous evening spent partying with friends.

As though aware of Maria's thoughts and content to remain disengaged, Dom casually lifted his leg to crack out a staggeringly long and wet fart. Maria immediately opened the driver's window of Dom's red Audi sports coupe and shot a look of horror his way. Dom responded by opening his window to gaze pensively at the barren moorland, reaching towards a distant, deep green tree line as his sausage roll-infused intestinal discharge caused a retching Maria to ease off the accelerator. Dom had insisted Maria drive today, as he was far too hungover to take the wheel.

Behind them, the road extended over farmland and rolling green hills to the motorway where their last utterances had been spoken. An argument in which everything had been left on the table, the remnants of which now harvested in the air between them as an unseen but palpable stain.

The road coughed up dust and fragments of grit as the car slowed to a halt on the side of the road. Maria switched off the engine and dropped her hands onto her lap defeatedly. The void between them charged with unsaid words and the flourishing odour of Dom's guts as they stared ahead at the road stretching away to a destination she hoped would save them.

\*

Dominic relished having the power. Although it would be easy for him to forgive Maria for something he wasn't even sure she had done, he had chosen not to trust her anymore, and that much was final. It was annoyingly and predictably clear to him that Maria wanted to give things another go and needed him to afford her a beacon of hope. But he wouldn't be held to ransom. Nor did he harbour any intention of allowing their relationship to survive the weekend; his scheme was quite simply to make Maria feel like shit. But he didn't want to show his cards just yet. Not when a trip to the country had already been planned for his birthday. No, he would see it to the end and, in the process, allow her to believe they would have a chance. And then, just as the weekend concluded, he would tell her to go fuck herself. A sentiment that was nothing less than she deserved in his world.

"Shall we just turn back?"

Maria's gentle tone carried a sadness she made no attempt to disguise. Dominic surmised all she craved was for him to dangle the proverbial piece of string, and he planned to allow her a last few strands of hope, of course, at his indulgence. Two hundred miles away from the bustling city life and into the country. To a place they had spent their first weekend together. A wooden cabin on a hill overlooked by a blue lake.

Within it was a bed where they had pleasured each other all weekend and a hot tub where they had watched the stars burst into life amongst the dark silence above. And the journey back, in that same car, when he touched her hand and whispered a promise of love to her. A shared murmur in both of their hearts. It seemed like a lifetime ago to Dominic, but it would make for a fitting and poetic end to their romance. With remnants of his flatus perfuming the air, he struggled to fight back his laughter before he spoke.

"Let's just get through this weekend and see what happens."

He intended for his gruff retort to carry just enough false sincerity for Maria to start the car again and continue along the road towards a place which held memories of a love she so desperately wished to keep hold of.

Dominic reached into his trouser pocket to retrieve his vibrating phone as the car rumbled back to life. Although Maria trusted him implicitly, he still angled his phone away to conceal the display. Unlike his past girlfriends, Maria had never once insisted on checking his phone to see who he was texting.

Suppressing a mocking chortle at her naivety, he scrolled down to a message from the girl he had fucked only last night, and his core warmed at the words on the screen, the same way it once had when things were good between Maria and him.

The message contained a response to his offer of a repeat performance after this *'charade of a weekend'*. Of course, Dominic had not shared with her the details of his weekend, that would be foolish! She was Scarlett, a redhead he met at a bar three weeks ago. A redhead who would likely have been way out of his league had it not been for his meticulous game.

Dominic now wasted no effort to conceal the excitement that flickered over his face at the memory. Dominic's game was relatively simple and built around the concept of appearing notably different from those he referred to as his competition. After experimenting tirelessly with various routines and outfits, he eventually perfected his demeanour. His persistent endeavours allowed him to sharpen his body language, empowering himself to subtly stand out from the crowd, usually by wearing a garish shirt, expensive shoes and well-fitting jeans. Standing out, or peacocking as Dominic affectionately called it, was relatively easy. The most challenging part of the game for Dominic was ignoring the pretty girls whilst the other idiots *(his competition)* in his vicinity ogled them without appreciating the consequence of their amateur and banal actions.

In his experience, pretty women were used to being desired, but they weren't used to being ignored.

*Those who stare get nowhere...*

Understanding this glitch in social dynamics, Dominic would carry out his measured charade until he decided upon his target for the evening, subtly, of course, and always using his friends as stooges. Dominic would fly under the radar, using a pre-rehearsed icebreaker on one of the less attractive members of the target's circle, always something non-threatening. Just to get them talking, and always paying no attention *(at first)* to the target. His default opener was always an opinion-based question—his motive conveniently disguised behind a non-intrusive enquiry about a fictitious event or unusual situation. In Dominic's experience, flying under the radar allowed him to disarm the target from the indignity of a predictable and direct approach. A direct approach brings a direct response, but a well-timed opener can subtly engage the remainder of the group. Dominic would remain indifferent to his target and even throw playful jibes at her when the opportunity presented itself. Of course, this system didn't always work. Still, Dominic's tireless practice ensured that he fine-tuned this technique, knowing when to move on and identifying when things were looking good for him, or as he called it, the green light. Failing all else and always as a last resort, Dominic could always speed the process by slipping *a little something* in their drink.

He relived the memory of noticing Scarlett on her own at the bar…

…Her deep red hair, crimson dress, and long, slender legs tapering into red heels drew him in like a moth to a flame. Dominic had somehow composed himself and tactically disregarded her presence against his natural impulses. He did this whilst subtly encouraging his friends to check her out. Later on, after a few had tried *(and failed)* to connect with her, he positioned himself beside her at the bar. He stood there for a while, observing her from his peripheral vision. It was so easy to see why women in bars held the power.

With the casualties of lust meeting his target from every angle, he could detect why women led the game and, more importantly, how he could use that game against them. His tireless practice told him that all he had to do was wait for the right moment.

To his surprise, Scarlett had accidentally bumped into him in an unexpected stroke of fortune, seemingly losing balance in her high-heeled shoes. Dominic remained in character *(practice makes perfect)* as he shot a polite smile her way and unloaded his favourite line about how comfortable her shoes looked. He confidently turned away to order a whiskey sour and watched her discreetly through the bar mirror, as she glanced down at her fashionable red high heels. She tried to regain his attention by hitting his arm playfully as hoped for and planned.

Dominic stood firm, unwilling to engage *(yet)* entirely in the exchange. Before he could conjure up a suitable retort, she had asked him his name and told him that he was notably different from his friends. Now off guard, Dominic turned to his friends, who were all ogling blatantly over, glaring wildly, and no doubt discussing whether Dominic was *in*.

Scarlett didn't appear troubled, and after a brief period of small talk, and with Dominic extending her the appropriate amount of eye contact, acting like the perfect listener, Scarlett finally accepted his offer to share some champagne with him. After one glass and noticing all the right signs from Scarlett, Dominic *(as planned)* attempted to end the interaction, but Scarlett was not keen to do so. Occasionally, he would walk off confidently to leave his conquest wanting more. As far as Dominic was concerned, he was James Bond. He often allowed the 007 theme music to frequent his mind as he walked away. On this occasion, however, he won what he gleefully referred to as a full closure of the deal. He had taken Scarlett back to his place, and things had gotten…interesting…

Those who stare get nowhere…

Dominic couldn't help but sigh dreamily as he reviewed the result of his social superpower and couldn't wait 'till his next night out with the boys to repeat his routine. He also could not wait for Scarlett to give him his real birthday present once he returned from his alleged lads' weekend away. She had asked him what he would like, and he had jokingly answered *"Anal*

*Sex"*. He expected to get another slap on the shoulder, as he had done when they met. Scarlett shocked him by answering cheekily, *"All right then"*.

As the car shook and rocked along the road, Dominic became aroused as he imagined Scarlett's soft, naked skin against his as he entered her for the first time and on the subsequent others before she left him alone to get ready for his weekend away. She seemed way out of his league, and Dom understood this to be the effect of his calibrated game. Or maybe Scarlett had a taste for older guys. He closed his eyelids to the memory of her removing that red, lacy underwear, her small breasts brushing against his smooth, taut chest as she slowly placed herself over him, her lips eager for his flesh. He could never resist a girl in red, but a redhead in red was a level-up for Dominic.

Placing the phone back into his pocket and making a mental note to ensure that he kept on top of his fitness this weekend to control his waistline, he glanced playfully at Maria, who, in response, smiled back with genuine devotion. He would think of Scarlett tonight as he fucked Maria, but not until Maria had effectively worked for his affection.

Practice makes perfect…

## CHAPTER TWO

Maria felt the electricity projected in Dom's gaze as he turned to her with a subtle glimmer of emotion. The sides of his eyes usually creased and twitched as he tried to conceal his feelings, and this caused an excited stirring to warm the coils of her stomach. It wouldn't be long before they reached the cabin, and she knew exactly what she would do when they arrived.

After an hour of rolling hills and thickening forest, the signpost for Lakeside Cabins emerged. Maria steered the car right onto a track, and the vehicle grumbled up a slight incline. Her attention was arrested by a prominent bulge stretching Dom's trousers. She immediately sped the car up the hill until the forest opened to a clearing, which served as a car park for the cabins.

Maria eased the car past the dimly lit reception

building and onto a narrow track behind the five wooden cabins adjacent to the oval lake, the surface of which shimmered and flickered gently under a scattering of raindrops. English oak trees towered side by side, facing the cabins. Their high-reaching branches, still flush with lime green leaves, dominated the sky above the campsite. Underneath the protective forest canopy, each cabin boasted a generous plot surrounded by a black picket fence. In front of the fence was a Privet hedge proudly displaying shiny green leaves, offering plenty of privacy for the hot tub on the decking. Maria noticed the cabins appeared vacant, with only darkness peering from windows, betraying no sign of life beyond the private wooden enclosures. The car's wheels crunched over stones and bumped across potholes as Maria slowed the engine on the clutch to the furthest of the five cabins—the most isolated plot.

Usually, at this time of year, it was relatively easy to get a booking, and by the look of the grey clouds which loomed over the lake, it was easy to see why. It occurred to Maria that they may have much more seclusion than she initially considered. And when those clouds finally wept, she and Dom would be encased together for the weekend, and she could make things right between them.

Maria manoeuvred the car along the path's conclusion and over the pebbled parking space for their private getaway. A high Cherry Laurel hedge concealed the cabin completely from its neighbouring structure.

Dom didn't acknowledge Maria, who turned to him expectantly as she switched the engine off. Instead, he headed straight for the trunk to reclaim their luggage. He carried both bags up the wooden steps and onto the decking towards the front door, which had a welcoming light above it, something which Maria hadn't acknowledged in the other cabins.

Maria took a few deep breaths before departing the car and following Dom to join him on the wooden decking. Her chest pounded as she reminisced about those memories shared on that first trip to the lake. These recollections pulled at her heartstrings, causing a rush of sickness to stir within her abdomen. Dom stood beside the door, affording her just enough room to squeeze past and use the key left in the lock for them to gain entry.

Inside, the lodge was generously spacious and

homely. A narrow hallway led through the middle of the cabin, with pictures of flowers and positive thoughts strewn over the walls. A double bedroom with an en suite was immediately on the right, and a second bedroom was at the end of the hall beside the entrance to the lounge area. Each wall was coated in warm red cedar, a theme which continued onto the wooden floor for much of the interior. Both bedrooms had thick, brown, shaggy carpets. The combined kitchen and lounge had two separate patio doors that opened onto the back decking with a lake view. Two large burnt leather reclining sofas faced a TV in front on the left side, and on the right was a well-equipped and modern kitchen with all the essentials required for a relaxing weekend away from civilisation.

The whole place was as she had remembered, and Maria didn't intend to waste any of their time together.

\*

Dominic observed Maria making her way into the main bedroom. Once there, she removed her hair band and sat earnestly on a double bed furnished tightly with plain white sheets underneath a green tartan blanket. Resisting the urge to smirk, he joined her in the room momentarily, and just as she reached out to him, he dumped her bag on the bed and made his way to the twin bedroom along the hallway. Once there, he placed his bag onto one of the single beds and located the charger for his phone, which was almost out of battery. After scrolling down and deleting the sexy pictures sent to him from Scarlett, he decided it was time to respond to her text. He couldn't leave her waiting too long.

*'Can't wait to see you on Monday night xxxx'*

After deleting the message *(just in case)*, he quickly dropped his phone onto the bed in reflex to the sound of Maria stirring behind him. He was about to indulge his moment of power by telling her to give him a bit of space, but his disposition changed when he saw what she was wearing. Or what she was not wearing, it was fairer to say. Maria stood under the doorway in nothing more than a flimsy red g-string. She held a complimentary bottle of Lakeside Cabin's champagne in one hand and two long-stem flutes in the other. Her short hair flowed generously atop her ample bare chest, licking at it like dark, sharpened tongues. Maria's slightly protruding stomach and smooth pale thighs looked sensational against the bright red lace that matched her blushing skin, and Dominic felt his guard drop as blood filled his loins. He couldn't resist a woman in red.

She knew him too well.

Maria turned and strolled back to the main bedroom, and Dominic followed without hesitation.

## CHAPTER THREE

Although Maria had wanted it to be a memorable reconnecting of their bodies, it hadn't been. She tried her best to assert control over Dom and slow down proceedings by pouring them a flute of champagne each and insisting cheekily that there would be no funny business until after their drinks. Dom had responded by necking both measures of fizz and stripping naked. He seemed more excited than usual, and after a few minutes of routine foreplay, Dom had ejaculated almost immediately after easing her red g-string to the side and entering her. Despite being nowhere near climax herself, she was *(at least)* content that she could turn him on. Now, she just had the remainder of the weekend to try and resolve things. She wanted to believe that he was worth just one more try. Still, it grated on her nerve how cold he had become recently, and her mind went into overdrive. She certainly wouldn't sleep tonight, but he had no fucking problem unwinding! As though in unsubtle acknowledgement of her thoughts, Dom twisted onto his front, cracked a sickeningly damp fart and resumed snoring blissfully.

Rolling out of bed with a defeated sigh and keen to disengage from the generous buffet of nose candy, Maria grabbed the bottle of champagne and headed to the hallway. She switched on the lamp and gently closed the door to the bedroom behind her, encasing it in darkness so as not to disturb Dom and his musical rectum. She knew he would be asleep for a while longer and wouldn't even be surprised if he slept 'till dawn. He'd been rather tired during the journey.

In the kitchen, Maria filled a coffee cup to the brim with champagne and exited through the sliding doors onto the patio. The outside lights illuminated a border around the wooden decking. Completely naked, she was thankful for the hedge's protective cloak of privacy to the hot tub in the centre of the enclosure, which she could hear rumbling invitingly under the cover. Beyond the balcony was a bank of uninterrupted grass that stretched forward to a lake, which no longer dominated the view as the gloom crept in. She sipped some champagne before placing her cup on the table beside the hot tub.

Maria's flesh raised in goosebumps in response to the breath of cold dusk air, but after lifting the hot tub lid, the steam enticed her into its welcoming embrace. The hot water reddened her skin as she eased in, closing her eyes and settling into its comforting warmth. Night met the wall of steam, making it impossible to see the lake, but she didn't care; she just wanted to try and switch off from the past week's events. With the bubbles massaging against her muscles, as though countless fingers tapping away at her aches and stresses, inside and out, she couldn't help but become utterly relaxed. For a moment at least, anyway, until those palpations probed deeper into her flesh, carrying invading thoughts of her current predicament into her mind.

She had loved Dom since the start.

When they met, Dom's overbearing confidence and indifference to an outfit she had spent hours deliberating over annoyed her. Still, it quickly transpired he wasn't like other men she had dated. For one, he was much older, but more importantly to Maria, Dom tuned in to her words, listening with absolute intent. He somehow made her feel special without telling her she was sexy, hot or any of the clique-ridden drivel that she often heard. They connected, and Maria fell willingly into his web of attraction.

She smiled as she recalled Dom's sarcastic comment about how comfortable her shoes had looked when she had gone to the trouble to wear them for anything but comfort. He also stated straight-faced that her favourite red dress was *'very nice'* and quite a popular choice for women these days. They had joked and laughed—she had even broken her first-date rule and allowed him to have sex with her. What followed for Maria, at least, was the best two years of her life.

Of course, it wasn't always sunshine and flowers; no relationship is without its imperfections. With Dom having to work away quite a lot, initially, their liaisons had been packed into the weekends. These were the best memories for her. Dom was always eager to see her when he stepped off the train and into her arms on Friday afternoons. Her embrace, in turn, became tighter and longer every time, especially on the painful goodbyes at the end of another fantastic few days with the man she considered marrying one day.

Maria's previous affiliations had never been much to shout about—a long string of wasted years, fixating on the wrong kind. As a teenager, she had more girlfriends than boyfriends. She couldn't bear to be alone. But now, one year to thirty, she had settled on the fact that she preferred the intimacy of male affection. Maria craved the attention of others and never had a bad word to say of her exes, which annoyed Dom, who often ranted, *"All guys are the same...they are just after one thing..."*

Maria leaned forward to switch off the bubbles and collect the champagne. The dim lights from the surrounding border around the decking made her think of Christmas. As she rested back in the tub, she breathed out measurably to subdue the tears pressing against the backs of her eyelids...

...Dom had travelled home to spend Christmas with his parents a couple of months after they got together, a routine he said would never change. Eager for a chance to finally meet his family, Maria had suggested that she come with him the following year. With her parents having passed away after a car accident when she was sixteen, she desperately craved the company of others. It was as if part of her had been lost, along with her parents.

*Maria simply couldn't function on her own.*

Dom was initially reluctant to change a routine that had served him well since childhood. However, Maria promised him the best Christmas ever, eventually persuading him to let her join him. It took great effort for her to be the perfect girlfriend in the months leading up to the festive season. To allow him to have his way during every petty argument they had. To not ask questions when he stayed out all night with his friends. She had even given in to his unflattering attempts at persuading her to try anal sex, which still caused her stomach to ache and crawl. Ultimately, after dropping an excuse on her at the last minute, he went home anyway and left Maria alone for Christmas.

*His parents probably didn't even know she existed.*

Maria trusted him implicitly and quite literally bent over backwards for him, but why couldn't he do the same for her?

After swallowing a mouthful of champagne, Maria replaced the cup on the table, then lay back in the warm embrace of the jacuzzi, running her arms back and forth through the water as she gazed at the stars above. She tried to clear her head, but something stirred amongst her thoughts. Maria was curious how much time Dom had been spending on his phone since their latest fallout just under a month ago…

…On Saturdays, Dom would go out to watch the football in one of the Irish bars in town. From there, he and his friends would move further into the city for their regular bar crawl before ending up in a nightclub.

Maria had called up some of her work colleagues and embarked upon their own girls' day out. She was often jealous of how much fun Dom had with his friends and felt they should be sharing each moment. So, after a few vodkas, she had purposefully led them to a pub she knew Dom frequented after the football had finished. She had even acted surprised to mask her organised interception when she met his friends, who were already half drunk. They were in high spirits because their football team had won, and they immediately noticed Maria at the entrance. Dom seemed happy to see her, although she deceitfully told him she didn't want to interrupt the boys' day out and that maybe she and her friends should go somewhere else. But she was wearing his favourite red dress, the one she had been wearing when they met, and the one he had later told her was the reason for him approaching her. Dom *(of course)* insisted they join them, much to the excitement of his notably younger friends, who eyeballed hungrily at Maria's companions.

Maria stretched out of the tub to fill another cup of champagne, which she gulped down, allowing the memory to continue painting itself on the backs of her eyelids…

…She wasn't much of a drinker, but Dom had insisted they all do shots, and soon, her capacity to remember much of the evening was lost in a blur of indecipherable chatter, flashing lights and thumping music. Her coherence returned to an argument with Dom at his flat afterwards. He was screaming at her for flirting with one of his friends, telling her she was acting like a slut in her '*red fucking dress*'. Maria had tried to argue back but, at the time, couldn't mentally replay the encounter. She had pleaded with him, completely out of character for her, but this was the man she loved. He was different from the rest. Dom eventually called a taxi and ushered her out of his flat, bellowing at her to *"Fuck off and go home"*.

Maria felt numb as she stood outside in her red dress and bare feet after accidentally leaving her shoes in Dom's flat. After a cold and uncomfortable wait, the taxi was nowhere to be seen, so Maria removed her phone from her bag, realising the battery had died. Turning to the intercom, she considered buzzing Dom. A moment of stubbornness overcame her, and she decided instead to walk towards town to try and flag a taxi for herself.

The recollection caused pain to swell in her chest, and Maria was met by a stifling sensation of panic, which spawned a cold chill to penetrate the warm embrace of the hot tub. Taking a long, deep breath, she allowed herself to slip entirely underwater, where she remained until she could bear it no longer. Maybe depleting her body of oxygen would quell the memory. Bursting out of the surface, gasping for air, she reached her shaking hand towards the bottle, necking a more significant gulp this time.

Reality raced back at her with the bitter taste of champagne. Like a stubborn echo unwilling to release its grip on Maria...

...As Maria walked towards town, she did so in silence. Cars slowed to observe her, eyes peering beyond darkened windows as she crossed the bridge connecting Dom's street to the town centre. Usually worried about getting attacked or lured into a taxi by a psychopath, on that occasion, she didn't care about anything. She couldn't bear the thought of being alone...*of starting again*...of going through the frivolities of dating to find another Dom...

...*She didn't want to be alive.*

At the centre of the bridge, Maria leaned on the railings and gazed down at the motorway as cars and trucks disappeared from view or burst into life—each vehicle with a purpose.

Each passenger on a journey.

Whether it was the experience with Dom, the excess alcohol, or her lack of direction in life, she did not know, but a hypnotic voice inside her head whispered...

...*just jump*...

*...just jump and make it all better...*

Maria noticed the tiny hairs on her skin reaching out to a stirring just behind her and the whisper of her name.

*...Maria...*

...Maria recognised this particular voice and immediately reconsidered jumping off the bridge.

It was Carmilla.

...The pulse in Maria's neck swelled, just as it had when she turned to see Carmilla stepping out of a taxi with a genuine look of concern on her face. Carmilla's silhouette dominated Maria's vision like an angel. She had only uttered three words, which seemed to have been simultaneously spoken in a trance from somewhere distant but nearby.

*Come with me...*

...The memory then filtered away into fragments Maria could not translate—a murmured haze of taking Carmilla by the hand, which closed tightly around hers. Followed by the world outside of a moving car, colours and lights racing and eventually fading to blackness. Next, Maria felt a cocktail of comfort and disorientation under a cold bed sheet. A warm body embraced her, the way a parent protects their child from the cold. Once again, her mind faded into oblivion until she awakened alone in bed as dust motes danced against the sun rays in front of her. It took her a moment to realise that her intercom had woken her.

In anticipation, Maria bounced out of bed to the intercom and held the button…

*"…Carmilla?"*

The voice which returned did not belong to Carmilla.

*"Who the fuck is Carmilla?"*

Maria buzzed Dom through without hesitation. Although she was slightly worried about seeing him, she was equally excited about telling him about her old friend.

Maria answered the door to be met with a furious Dom. He projected a malice so sincere that she expected him to hit her. He had never once raised a fist to her, but she had previously never seen this side of him. Gritting his teeth together, his cheeks red with anger, he remained quiet as he stormed past Maria into her flat.

All was evident to Maria as she organised her

thoughts. The recollection brought a sickening sensation of impending dread, which had begun to exert itself on her nerves. She reached for the champagne bottle and swallowed a few more mouthfuls. A drink typically associated with celebration now nearly choked her as she coughed out heavily and sucked in the cold night air…

…Dom had waited until the door was closed before walking over to the sofa and sitting regally in its centre.

*"I will ask you this once. And I will know if you are fucking lying. Where the fuck have you been?"*

Maria feared his reaction and knew she could not say anything to quell his threatening tone. So, she told him the truth.

*"I have been here…sleeping."*

His eyes fixated on her, unblinking and full of malice.

*"Sleeping, eh? Or fucking this Carmilla? Isn't she that ex-girlfriend you told me about? And what kind of name is that, anyway?"*

*"Jesus…Dom…come on!"*

Dom stood abruptly from the sofa and rushed

towards her. She flinched for a second, but he didn't touch her. Instead, he shot past her and departed the flat with a slam of the door. In the days afterwards, he ignored her efforts to make contact. Maria spent much of that time alone until Dom appeared at her front door a week later. He had been out drinking with his friends and told Maria he was sorry and had begun to realise how much he missed her. Maria opened the door to him, and later on, she even opened her legs for him. Once satisfied, Dom passed out beside her, snoring as usual.

Dom awoke the following day and regretted coming over. He wasn't angry but told Maria he couldn't trust her anymore. That's when Maria told him precisely what had happened: that she was innocent, that Carmilla was looking out for her because he had left her out in the cold. But that wasn't enough for Dom.

*"Cheating is cheating. Whether it's with a girl or a guy. And you don't seem to have a preference, do you, you little slut?"*

The words cut her profoundly, weakening her resolve. His rejection had poisoned her so potently that she couldn't even remember who she was before meeting him. She had cried as she told him how much *shit* she had put up with for Christmas so that she could finally meet his parents. Dom had just stood up once more and attempted to leave the flat. She couldn't figure out why she had decided to hold onto him, to try and stop him from going. She even pleaded with him, on her hands and knees, to give her just one chance.

*Just who the hell was she anymore?*

And it was at that moment she had given up on her sense of self-worth.

Maria took another deep breath and submerged into the water. This time, she didn't plan on resurfacing. She recalled reading somewhere that it was impossible to drown yourself willingly, but she was ready to give it a damn good try.

Maria tuned in to the murmuring recesses of silence among the void beneath the bubbles. The outside world was now blurred under a warm mask of steam. Maria's pulse rose quickly as she forced herself to tune out from reality. But she was alone, desperately alone. No one awaited her amid the shifting and twisting lights, which faded as her heart slowed.

Maria panicked aggressively for oxygen. She

convulsed as a reflex caused her to slide her feet against the bottom of the hot tub. The noise of her skin sliding against the base produced a vibration that filled her ears, and she burst out from the water to inhale a mixture of steam and cold air. She then managed to slowly gain control of her breathing as she thought of Dom's demeanour in the car from only a few hours earlier. There had been a complete change in his attitude towards her as soon as his phone vibrated. Just as the plastic flooring had vibrated in her ears, whispering its secrets, maybe the phone had betrayed his.

Maria slowly exited the tub and returned to the lodge, hoping Dom was still asleep.

## CHAPTER FOUR

As expected, Dom was fast asleep. Maria knew that by now, there would be no waking him until morning. His ability to crash out in the seconds after sex used to grate on her, but tonight, it served as a blessing. Dom's phone was plugged into the twin bedroom wall, and he was unconscious in the master bedroom. After a cursory glance behind her, she uncoupled the handset, grabbed one of the courtesy robes and quietly re-entered the lounge area. She was damp underneath the dressing gown but still tingled with warmth from the hot tub.

Settling into one of the two reclining sofas, she pressed the home button, and the screen displayed a passcode lock. She quickly keyed in Dom's year of birth. Having watched him discreetly over the past few months, she knew he used the same code for all his passwords. His bank pin, his laptop, and, of course, his phone.

With the phone unlocked, she felt her heart rate accelerate as she navigated his messages and photos. Several moments of scrolling revealed nothing out of the ordinary, no hidden messages, and no pictures of naked women. She was then overcome by a sense of guilt for invading his privacy. However, her disposition altered when a message flashed from a contact named SCARLETT.

*'I can't wait to see you, either. You had better save your energy for me xx'*

Maria dropped the phone onto the sofa and sat in silence. In front of her, the patio window reflected her pale complexion. Beyond, the hot tub glowed a warming shade of amber, which caused the hair in her doppelganger to gleam a strange shade of crimson. She could just about hear the pump rumble as she sat there like a statue. The only movement betrayed by her reflection was her slowly rising and falling shoulders.

*How fucking dare he?*

Her mind was ablaze as everything suddenly fell into place—his reluctance to make an effort with her, his short temper. And she had allowed him to walk all over her and accuse her of cheating and fuck her in the ass when he was receiving a full turndown service from fucking Scarlett.

After taking a slow, measured breath to steady her nerves, she picked up the phone again and opened the last message. Before she could stop herself, she began to respond.

*'I don't think I can wait to see you… If you are not busy, let's hook up this weekend xx'*

Maria knew she had crossed a line, and as a chill ran under her scalp, she shuddered. This was grossly uncharacteristic of her, and she could only blame her actions on the surprisingly potent effect of the alcohol. Dom's phone vibrated lightly in her hand as she sat silently, contemplating her subsequent endeavours. Panicking, she nearly dropped the handset. After clicking the switch for silent mode, she read the message.

*'I thought you were with the guys xx?'*

Her heart burned in pain at the level of Dom's deceit. Impulse now took control of her faculties as she began her response…*his* response, as her eyes overflowed with water.

*'That has fallen through. We booked a lodge, but the guys have pulled out, and I am stuck here on my lonesome xx'*

She expected the deceit to be recognised, having yet to learn exactly what he had told Scarlett about the weekend. One thing was sure: he hadn't told her he was away for a romantic make-or-break weekend with his fucking girlfriend.

The screen lit up again, and Maria's mouth went dry.

*'Seriously! Wow! How can I say no to that?? Well… I can come over, as long as it's not too far away xxx'*

Maria felt a cold shiver tearing through her insides—an inaudible warning of the potential outcome if she took things any further. Her heart's dull thud intensified as she pictured Dom denying everything and leaving her alone…

…alone again…

The pulsations in her chest synchronised into a deeper strand of her essence. Drumming a rhythmic whisper to her subconscious that no matter what happened from this point on, she couldn't allow Dom to leave her.

*'It's Lakeside Cabins. It's quite a drive from town, but I promise it will be worth it. We even have a hot tub! Xxx'*

Maria clenched her jaw as she sent the message and wiped the tears from her cheeks. Should this bitch make an appearance, it would be worth it. To see the look on Dom's face. There would be no condemning her this time around. He would indeed be caught, red-handed. Then she could deal with him and whoever that bitch was!

The subsequent response took a few minutes. With her guts twisting, she waited for the screen to glow.

*'Okay. You had better make sure that the tub is nice and warm. I can call you when I arrive tomorrow, or you never know... maybe I will surprise you earlier xxx'*

Maria could hear her heart booming in her ears. Panic began to creep up on her, and her skin tingled with static as she contemplated her plan. Jesus, what plan? She needed to figure out what she was doing. But then, a moment of clarity. Her hands shook with anticipation as she typed in the last message.

*'No. Don't call. My phone is just about to go on the blink, and I forgot my charger. Just go to reception, and they can*

*let me know you have arrived. I can't wait to see you xxx'*

Maria didn't want to risk Scarlett's arrival at the cabin just in case she was asleep and missed the show, as she was starting to feel increasingly tired.

Scarlett's reply was swift.

*'LOL… That's fine. Sleep well, my angel… See You Later xx'*

With her stomach rising to fill her throat, Maria grew nauseous and had to take another deep breath to compose herself.

*Sleep well, my angel… Who the fuck says that?*

Standing up slowly, she deleted the messages as she walked, but she didn't plan for Dom to have a chance to open his phone. After scrolling through his settings, she changed his password to a random set of numbers. Next, she returned outside and fully submerged his phone in the hot tub. She held it under the massaging bubbles until the light switched off before removing it and trying to switch it on again. The phone was dead. And even if he managed to salvage it, it would take him a while to figure out how to bypass the password lock.

Back inside the cabin, she plugged the phone into

its charger, placing it onto one of the single beds while she sat on the other to finish the remaining champagne. A surge of rage unexpectedly manifested in the silence.

"I will cut his dick off and feed it to him."

Maria's breath misted into the night and out of the window vent. And with those words silently evaporating into the air, she experienced her anger dissolving, as did the alcohol in her bloodstream. Maria couldn't recall ever having such a violent thought in her life. Still, she couldn't ignore the exhilaration that carried those malevolent notions of exacting vengeance against Dom.

She could hear Dom snoring, and as she guzzled back the contents of the bottle, the warm flush of alcohol met her. Satisfied at the evening's work and that Dom would soon have to answer for his infidelity, Maria yielded to the tightening grip of sleep as a peculiar weakness washed over her. A stubborn notion came with the tiredness that her abject fear of being alone may never leave her, no matter what she did, and this certainty terrified her more than facing the truth of what Dom had been up to.

Just as she was about to switch off the light, she

realised it would be easy enough to work out that water damage had ruined his phone. With that in mind, she got herself a cup of water from the lounge, noticing how heavy her head had suddenly become. Back in the room, she emptied the cup on the bed and laid it by the phone. When Dom woke up and immediately went for his phone, which she knew he would, he would assume it had been damaged by accident.

Marvelling at her stroke of genius, Maria closed her eyes with a smile. It didn't strike her as odd at the time why sleep embraced her so quickly. Nor did she resist the deep and welcoming darkness which draped over her like a burial shroud fashioned by the silence. Underneath the gentle drum of what sounded like a thousand nails entombing her in the cabin, Maria drifted helplessly into the abyss.

## CHAPTER FIVE

Maria could not be sure how long she had slept.

The groan of distant thunder rocking the sky awakened her. As she tuned in to the escalating drum of rainfall on the cabin roof, she envisioned the sound to be the tapping of countless frantic hands, desperate for respite from the arriving storm. Cocooned amongst the encasement of her duvet wrapped tightly around her, it took her a short while to orient herself to the surroundings. The dull warning of a headache loomed, causing Maria to stir, as did the need for a cold drink.

Her attention was drawn to the bed beside her, confirming Dom must have crept through upon waking to reclaim his phone. The bed had a damp patch on its white duvet cover, and the charger remained plugged into the wall. But it was the stillness within her vicinity that bothered her the most. It was as if her actions from the night before spoiled the atmosphere, intoxicating it with a palpable sense of impending dread.

Easing up from the bed, her temple violently filled with blood. The sensation proved too much for her dehydrated body, and she had to sit back down to prevent keeling over. After a few steadying efforts, she finally managed to stand. The carpet was warm underneath her bare feet, but as she made her way into the hallway, she identified several wet patches which were cold against her skin. Ignoring them momentarily due to her vision blurring out much detail, she made for the kitchen to quench her unrelenting thirst, expecting to be met with an enraged Dom demanding to know what had happened to his phone. Or even worse, if he had somehow switched his phone on and unlocked it, he would have plenty more to enquire about. Maybe that fucking Scarlett bitch had arrived when she was sleeping, and Dom had managed to get rid of her.

*Jesus, just how long had she crashed out for?*

Maria considered this. They had got to the lodge late afternoon, so she estimated that she must have fallen asleep around nine or ten in the evening. From the modest glint of dawn outside, Maria assumed she must have slept right through the entire night. She tried to recall where she had left her phone so that she could check the time. She was sure she had left it in the room with Dom.

The lounge area was empty. No, not empty, devoid of life, perhaps. Or at least that's how Maria perceived the stirring and unnerving sensation. The unnatural quiet began to grate on her. The rain was now a blur over the patio windows, adding to the sudden claustrophobia that overwhelmed her like a dense, weighted blanket.

"Dominic...Dom?"

Maria's voice sounded unfamiliar, as if her words had come from someone else. Shaky and high-pitched. The lack of any response unsettled her gravely. No longer concerned about being faced with a raging soon-to-be ex-boyfriend, she grimaced against her pulsing headache, departed the lounge, and stood in the hallway to listen for any sounds. Maybe he was fast asleep. As an annoyingly restless sleeper, she would have awakened to anyone arriving at night. Still, the air was tainted by a presence that now shared the cabin with her, but why couldn't she hear anything stirring from within that room?

Maria approached the door with caution. For fear of Dom furiously bursting out of the room towards her, she stealthily crept towards the place she had left him snoring and gripped the handle. Her heart rate intensified as her mind raced through the sight she would soon behold behind that door.

Maria carefully opened the door to a room smothered in a black shroud. Not a shadow passed the threshold, but she knew something was terribly wrong as the hairs on her neck reached out towards an unseen presence lurking amid the dark void.

With trepidation, Maria flicked the switch to illuminate the enclosure.

The dull glow tracked over a large mound beneath the duvet cover, once white but now stained red at two prominent points. Maria was invaded by a profound unease about the mass encased within that shroud of linen.

The truth was finally revealed as she grabbed the end of the duvet and pulled it firmly towards her.

Dom was naked underneath her stare, and her disbelieving eyes took a moment to adjust to the spectacle before her. It was clear he wasn't breathing. No rising or falling of the chest occurred, nor did any sound of life stir in the musty air. His eyes were wide, empty voids embedded in a face frozen with panic and fear.

Due to Dom's position, his head hung backwards over the side of the bed. There looked to be an object jammed into his mouth, but she couldn't quite make out what, as the sudden light had blurred her vision. But as her sight accustomed to the scene, she became captivated by a triangular gaping wound at his groin, where much of the blood had begun to thicken.

*I will cut his dick off and feed it to him…*

Maria's hand covered her mouth to prevent the words from manifesting, but it was too late. Her eyes were now fixed on the pulsating red tissue that trembled in Dom's throat. Was it…moving?

She stood defiantly poised at the doorway, struggling to maintain her cognition and balance, wishing the scene in front of her to be a dream. The carpet rose as her feet gave way to knees that crumpled under the dead weight of her limp body, piling in awkwardly on the threshold where she now gazed up at

Dom's impossibly positioned head. The pain and terror echoing in those two vacant wounds was too much for her to suffer with any deliberate effort. One last laboured breath drew in little sustenance from the air, which seemed starved of oxygen. As the world swam away across the ocean of her awareness, the last thing Maria saw was the writing on the ceiling above Dom's corpse in what could only be his blood, smeared with attentive strokes.

THOSE WHO STARE GET NOWHERE!

*

*Dominic knew it had to be a dream.*

*As angelic as his visitor was, he doubted whether even she could float above him, beckoning him with eyes more beautiful than he had ever seen. Her silk dress, the red one he loved, flowed softly over her curves, and he could see the outline of her nipples piercing the thin fabric. Inviting but out of reach. He ogled her red high-heeled shoes, which she had worn when they met, and his loins pulsated. His subconscious mind presented no return journey to reality, but he didn't care. This was getting interesting, so he allowed the dream to take him further. From below, he could see his erection rising proudly towards red lips, which parted to take him. He watched as her red hair shrouded his throbbing penis from sight, and her soft, warm tongue worked him gently, at first, teasingly, but then more earnestly. He almost called out, but she stopped what she was doing and pressed her finger firmly against the lips he so wanted to fuck. But why couldn't he move? Dismissing this notion, he pleaded silently for her to continue, and soon, he was back inside her mouth, pulsating and sliding back and forth. His pleasure was joined by a kaleidoscope of all of his past conquests, their naked bodies clambering atop each other, born through memories he would hold dearly forever. Clay for him to mould into whatever he pleased whenever he sought pleasure. He remembered the smell of them and the way their cheap perfumes yielded to the taste of their excitement as his mouth overflowed with saliva. They writhed and moaned in ecstasy, and his thoughts turned to Maria for a second as he neared orgasm. He did love her, in his weird way, but he loved new pussy more than anything else and would do whatever it took...*

*The pleasure ceased abruptly, and a tightening spasm radiated from his genitals, followed by a tremendous pressure which sprayed deep into the cavern which had only moments ago pleasured him. She raised her head, and he urgently sought an escape from this nightmare. Instead, he could feel himself increasingly drawn away from any safety beacon. She smiled at him, but the fountain of cascading crimson showering over her face and breasts worried him gravely. If this was a dream, why was the pain so intense?*

*Holding her gaze, he tried to shake himself awake rather than observe the catalyst of this fountain that had painted her skin. The crimson licks of blood contrasted against the soft brush of her red hair like paint being flicked onto a canvas.*

*Realising no respite was forthcoming, he tried to prise himself from the bed, but once again, she brought her long finger to her mouth to silence him. He helplessly obeyed as an excruciating level of agony threatened to split him in half. She removed his still-twitching penis from her mouth, and it was then that he felt the blood pooling under his body. His efforts to scream brought no sound. Nor did his desperation bring forth any mercy. He was utterly devoid of strength to respond in any way to the violence.*

*She leered gleefully at him, slowly sliding up his frame, carrying his moderately pumped-up cock, offering it up to his wide-open mouth. He wrestled with his subconscious to break free from this terror, but now she was floating again, whispering to him in a voice that couldn't have been human.*

*"Now you get to see what you have been missing."*

*She thrust his dismembered penis into his mouth, all the way into his throat and watched him as he shuddered wearily in acceptance of his fate. He could distinguish the cloying bitterness of his blood, which blended with the salty thickness of his semen. He gagged violently, but this only caused her sneer to widen.*

*"It tastes nice, huh? I don't want you to worry; this is just the beginning of your birthday surprise."*

*As Dominic convulsed, she positioned her leg above him to display a shiny metallic stiletto heel.*

*"Remember these shoes, baby? The ones you told me that look so comfortable?"*

*Dominic tried again to scream but had no power to operate his mouth, nor could he move his faculties. Choking and vomiting on the twitching instrument of his past pleasures, he strained once again but could not control his limbs. Why couldn't he wake up?*

*She slowly and carefully ran the long, sharp, serrated metal heel across his face, teasing him with its intended purpose.*

*"Now, what did you ask me for... Anal, wasn't it?"*

*Her foot disappeared from view, and a searing pain filled Dominic's rectum, followed by a gushing fluid which soaked his backside. The sensation was replaced by the most excruciating agony twisting through his guts as the heel was shoved in and out with violent, crushing thumps.*

*"Please tell me, how comfortable do these shoes feel now?"*

*The ordeal did not fold to Dominic's prayers, nor did the intensity of the suffering relent. His vision had all but diminished, but he could now see her silhouette looming above him on the bed, with one leg raised high. A hideous brown and red fluid spillage lashed from the heel's serrated edge, lubricated entirely with his intestinal sinew.*

*With the storm battering the windows and the cabin walls groaning under the strain, Dominic wailed silently as the serrated razor heel blade came down firmly, puncturing his eye and piercing deep into his skull with a violent crunch. When the heel was driven home into his second ocular cavity, Dominic faded into a flooding darkness, which welcomed him into its cold and bitter embrace, and his existence finally yielded into the abyss.*

## CHAPTER SIX

The air was still as Maria opened her eyes to the bitter chill of reality. Scattered recollections of what had taken place before she passed out quickly invaded her thoughts, and with a panicked and laboured effort, she turned onto her side and glanced again into the bedroom in a helpless endeavour to satisfy her wish for all of this to have been a dream. Under the glow of daylight, she assessed the viciously adulterated body of Dom. His skin was pale white with a tinge of blue. His savagely bludgeoned eyeholes were brutally torn to display a deep shade of bottomless crimson. Maria estimated that whatever tool had been used was used violently and with an artist's precision, similar to the neatly blood-painted message on the ceiling…

…THOSE WHO STARE GET NOWHERE…

Maria swore she remembered those words from

somewhere but couldn't arrange her ruminations to establish where or when. As she tried desperately to forge an understanding of her current situation, a sudden pain seared into her chest. With each laboured breath she took, the suffering amplified. Maria struggled to find oxygen in the air and felt herself sinking into the floor as the colour drained from her surroundings and a sharp ringing tone grated through her skull.

Maria worked her jaw to relieve the tension afflicting her head, her breathing increasingly constricted as the world around her took on an ominous and threatening presence. She could feel her organs shutting down as the atmosphere pressed upon her. From her peripheral vision, it looked as though a sheet of static danced over the bed, the walls, and Dom. An escalating high-pitched sound crashed into the soft recesses of her brain. She tuned in to every sensation inside and outside her…and then…she breathed. As oxygen flooded her lungs, it did so with a sense of euphoria at the kiss of life, almost with a newfound respect for her limbs, flesh, and choices.

Fascinated by this odd and unexpected turn of

events, she was abnormally calm. Emotion no longer seemed to burden her, and rather than scream for help, she remained motionless as she listened for signs of any movement within the lodge.

After a while, she was content that the stillness of the lodge was uninterrupted. It occurred to her that whoever had visited the lodge had likely done so for Dom alone before disappearing to let Maria deal with the aftermath and possibly even face the blame. It just had to be whoever she sent those texts to. The only other option was that Maria had fallen into a psychological break and killed Dom herself. Although she appeared numb, the thought of Dom, now unable to corrupt her mind, began to worry her.

*Everyone fucking leaves me in the end...*

Maria carefully got to her feet and analysed the room for her phone. She remembered leaving it in her jacket on the chair, but after checking the pockets, she presumed that her phone must have been taken. She departed the room and followed the hall into the kitchen to satisfy her urgent craving for a cool drink. As she held a cup below the faucet, she became disconcerted at the peculiar disposition that had replaced her apparent shock response, which had caused her to faint only a few hours earlier.

She replaced the cup under the faucet after guzzling its contents, repeating this procedure until the water ran from the sides of her mouth. Maria envisioned she was a vampire and that the liquid saturating her robe was the blood of her latest victim. Hell, if she had indeed feasted on the cock of that fucking bastard Dom, it wouldn't have been for the first time!

She laughed strangely at her morbid joke and once again was concerned about her unnatural reaction to the brutally disfigured corpse, which lay several feet away, now only partially covered by its white burial shroud.

It was as she placed the cup in the sink that she saw the blood on her hands. And not just her hands. Her arms and legs were stained in a dried glaze of crimson slick that she hadn't noticed before.

*Maybe she didn't want to...*

In fact, after assessing the hallway floor, it occurred to her that the wet sensation underneath her feet was undeniably blood. Dried footprints of blood had congealed on the carpet and wooden floor, and their direction was clear. The imprints of someone's tread betrayed a journey from where Dom lay to where Maria had slept, blissfully unaware of the sadism being inflicted on him.

*Or was she...*

Appreciating the hollow emptiness inside her and a reluctance to portray any emotion, she lifted her arm in front of her. Not once was her movement met with any resistance or, indeed, any shaking. And it wasn't just that. Her heart rate was steady, poised. In the absence of any physical symptom of her appalling plight, her gaze now fixed on the stains of red, which had dried deeper on the slicked hairs of her arm. Sensing disgust at these stains, she immediately removed her robe, discarding it where she stood, and walked calmly into the bathroom, where she had a long warming shower.

After her shower, she had to work stealthily not to tread on the blood-stained footprints and drippings that marked the wooden floor beneath her bare feet. During this game of stepping stones, a laugh interrupted the silence. It took her a few moments to realise that the gleeful cackling came from her excited mouth.

Alongside the vibrations of her unexpected amusement came a stirring within her—a compulsion which grew in severity with the command that she should probably head to the park reception and contact the police. Panic trapped the laughter in her throat—a vivid recollection of her actions. A peculiar, broken memory of the bloodshed and of Dom cowering as the crimson remains of his life rained down over his naked body. Her anxiety yielded abruptly to bouts of laughter. Was she capable of committing such an act? She had read of people doing unspeakable things after a severe psychological break.

*Could this really have happened to her?*

With the storm gathering momentum outside, Maria decided that whatever the catalyst for Dom's current position, there was nothing she could do here, with no phone and likely no visitors in the neighbouring cabins. If the lodge reception was still open, she could collect her thoughts and have a stiff drink to take the edge off. Then, all would become apparent, and she would know what to do for the best.

Maria returned to her dead boyfriend's tomb,

treading carefully around the blood stains, the child-like charade once again delighting her, causing her efforts to falter at the suppression of hysterical giggling. Ignoring the carnage left behind by whatever monster had feasted on his rotten, cheating and brainless cock, she chuckled to herself as she searched her bag to find an appropriate outfit to wear. Her gaze drew up to the congealing message inscribed on the ceiling in his blood, like a morbid epitaph.

### THOSE WHO STARE GET NOWHERE!

Why couldn't she ascertain where she had heard those words? One thing was for sure, though—she cackled—whoever had committed this obscene act had a twisted sense of humour.

As the storm continued its approach and the cabin jostled under the breath of its arrival, Maria replaced any residual notion of calling for help with a strange certainty...that when the storm finally arrived, it carried something in its song, just for her...

## CHAPTER SEVEN

Justin couldn't wait to close the bar and fuck off home. Due to the foul weather warning, several guests had cancelled their bookings yesterday, just in time for the midday cut-off. Much to Justin's disappointment, one of those cancellations was a hen night.

As well as giving Justin little to anticipate, it also meant they didn't get charged. In his opinion, this was financial suicide for a small business like Lakeside Cabins. But what did he care? The owner didn't! Since Justin had taken the job on after being released from prison, the place had gone to shit. He scoffed and remembered his interview for the job. He turned up in his best charity shop two-piece suit, worried that no one would employ someone on the sex offenders register. With no forthcoming applicants having an appetite to work in such a remote area, no travel allowance, and minimal wage, he was employed just for showing up.

Upon commencing employment, he was stressed out that with due diligence, his offer would be redacted after the appropriate checks had been made. But here he was, almost two years later. The barman and receptionist of a place where families came to relax for the weekend and where people came to fuck; a place which lent itself perfectly to Justin's inherent need to look…to stare…and to think of all the things he would love to do, to all those girls.

*Justin just loved to stare…*

It only took him a month of employment before he returned to his old ways. He would scrutinise the list of those arriving and find the best place for his cheap black and white hidden camera to monitor the intended target. He had to be careful, as on occasion, he had been visited by the local policeman who was friends with the owner, a stern and reserved man who made it clear he didn't trust Justin.

Nevertheless, Justin had developed a fine-tuned perception of exactly where he could place the camera, and the rewards had undoubtedly been fruitful. From watching married couples have awkward and silent sex in the spooning position, not to wake their kids, to sometimes teenage daughters quietly masturbating. But what Justin liked most was the agreement he and his old friend Dominic had held since they reconnected when he got out of prison.

Dominic was a piece of shit, but he was never short of pussy. He would contact Justin routinely, who in turn would grant Dominic a free stay at the lodge as long as Justin got a ringside seat, either by setting up a camera or peering through a crack in the door, as Dominic got to work on his new squeeze.

Of course, Dominic would never allow this to occur for his steady girlfriends. It was a fuckbuddy-only agreement, but Justin had gone ahead and set up a camera in the bedroom in a location unknown to Dominic. The internet was poor at the cabin, meaning he couldn't enjoy a live show. Additionally, the camera was of inferior quality and had to be set on a timer to save the battery. But once Dominic left, Justin would at least *(hopefully)* have something to look forward to.

Keeping his recordings offline was much less risky anyway—a far cry from back when they took many more risks. After Justin was released from prison, Dominic told him about this place and that it was an ideal scouting post for someone with appetites like theirs.

Justin stood up from behind the bar, catching a glimpse of his reflection in a mirror bordered by hanging glasses and dust-topped bottles. When he was in prison, he had got himself in decent shape, but now the image cast back was of a man at least twenty years older than his thirty-nine times orbiting the sun. His grey flannel shirt hung off his shoulders in folds but clung tightly to his generous midsection. His loose-fitting trousers did little to disguise his skinny legs, and he sighed heavily at an appearance which served to offer no attraction to the opposite sex. He had shaved his hair off for two reasons. The first was that his hair was getting grey. The second was that he didn't ever want anyone to recognise him from his past.

Back in the day, Justin sampled every form of indulgence until he found his preferred role as a bystander who encouraged his friends to partake in whatever debauchery presented itself. Whether that be pleasuring himself in public areas or recording his friends taking turns with a girl who had, let's say, had too much to drink…

He was eventually imprisoned for a modest *(in his opinion)* misdemeanour after installing cameras in the changing room at the local gym so he could watch the young girls getting ready for dance practice.

Justin picked up his phone to check the time, sighing heavily that he had at least six hours left of his shift. He had been advised to stay in reception until ten p.m. in case anyone was stupid enough to venture out here with a storm forecast. Still, with only one cabin occupied by Dominic *(who had informed Justin to keep his perverted eyes to himself)* and his latest conquest, Justin decided he may risk it and piss off upstairs to bed early.

He was barely out of his seat to start closing the bar down when the chime above the front door indicated the arrival of a guest. Justin swore under his breath, but his disposition quickly changed as a young woman, dark hair drenched wet against a tired but pretty face, crossed the threshold. His gaze tracked curves betrayed by a wet red dress, which smoothed over her ample figure and sent blood racing to his extremities. Although it seemed unlikely Justin was getting an early night, maybe things were about to get interesting.

*

Maria couldn't remember getting dressed, nor could she recall her journey from the cabin to the reception where she now sat. She had to piece the puzzle together somehow and execute a plan. If it turned out to be her that killed Dominic, then so be it.

Maria felt her shoulders shrugging again in a helpless reflex as laughter overtook her at the thought of Dom's current situation and the certainty that his cheating days had come to an end. Fuck, she needed help. But more than anything, and before she potentially faced a prison sentence, she needed a stiff drink.

Lakeside Cabins reception itself was a cabin. Larger in size than the residential cabins, which eased and groaned at the now unrelenting rain pummelling on the wooded exterior. She could hear the wind whistling through the trees and bushes outside, singing a melody as it found gaps and joists in the outer shell of the enclosure. Maria was drawn to the cry of the rain as it flickered over the roof in sheets and imagined that an ushered warning was being carried about the approach of something terrible. She couldn't help but enjoy the burning sensation of countless scalding rain droplets as they melted into her skin in response to the dry heat. The sound of the crackling embers of the coal fire conveyed its own ushered warning, as did the loud clunk of a grandfather clock which was positioned beside the front door, as though a stationary ever-watching guardian in the tomb of wooden walls and leather armchairs.

With the storm increasing in magnitude, Maria's heart began to flutter in anticipation that within its aggressive onslaught was her fate. The violent weather battering the campsite meant that only she and the repulsive barman frequented the cosy interior of the pub.

It didn't matter that the barman's demeanour betrayed an intrinsic motive for his kindness in serving her at the table in the corner of the lounge. His dishevelled appearance gave off no sense of threat. Nor did his overbearing curiosity bother Maria. The attention caused her to feel alive. She wasn't used to anyone noticing her, and the shock of what had happened in the cabin had stirred up an internal musing that maybe she didn't even exist.

*Could that be true?*

She allowed herself to explore what the world would look like as a ghost. She may as well be one. No one ever seemed to regard her, and everyone fucking left her... But then, would the barman's gaze steady on her with such silent understanding if she were indeed merely a formless entity? Maria could feel his irises peeling off her clothes. His eyes slid over her like maggots, squirming their way into rotten meat.

Maria had bigger fish to fry, though. As her mind blazed with what she could only describe as madness, she allowed the soothing burn of straight vodka to work its way into her furthest recesses.

Suppressing chortling laughter once more at the image of Dom, she raised her empty glass at the barman, who reluctantly nodded and poured another vodka. He was a tall, portly man, probably in his early 50s, with deep lines of bitterness and age carved into his sallow flesh. With the careless clunk of ice dropping into her drink, Maria watched as her servant approached the table, the light from the fireplace beaming off his hairless head. He scanned casually over the wet clothing which clung to her frame; he either thought she hadn't noticed or didn't care if she did.

*Those who stare get nowhere!*

The words that had worried her from earlier, written in blood above the corpse of Dom, now began to harvest an idea. A way out of this mess for her, if she could somehow pin all of this mess...on someone else...

"On your own tonight, *Miss*?"

Miss... The tone carried sarcasm, but she did not acknowledge his futile efforts to exert any dominance. She settled instead to meet his comment with a smile and a slow nod. She didn't even realise how intently she was grinning until the barman's expression relinquished to a flustered frown.

"I was meant to close early tonight, but I am happy to keep you company and *serve* you for the evening. Everyone else looks to have been wise enough to stay away. Only you and Dominic are booked in for the weekend. There's a storm coming."

He returned reluctantly to the bar, breathing a sigh of frustration as he left Maria at the table. Maria, in turn, felt her skin crawling.

*Did he just say only you and Dominic?*

Shit…fuck…shitfuck!

That left Maria with an even more significant problem to deal with: The barman's knowledge of Dom, whether or not that was just because he knew the names of those booked in. It didn't matter either way. Maria had to think. Her synapses fired like a steam train, generating vivid memories she did not recognise. But it wasn't just that; her entire disposition was unfamiliar to her…unnatural. Things just didn't seem real.

Maria knew she had to organise her thoughts and start making harsh decisions, but did she carry the sanity she once had before all of this? It occurred to her that she couldn't recall much beyond her and Dom on the road to the cabin, as though a huge chunk of her mind was being eaten away by the same maggots spilling from the barman's lecherous gaze. Maybe the wave of shock from the scene in the cabin was washing over her, eventually rinsing her away to no more than a dribbling mess. Paranoia crept up in crunching waves, causing her to shiver, as did the notion that if this barman stared at her once more, maybe she would remove those eyes from his fucking skull.

Another smile crept across Maria's face as the vodka filtered into her blood, clearing away the residue of her worry. The warm glow of alcohol created a perplexing cocktail of emotion, and with the rain and wind shaking the foundations of the world outside, something told her that everything was going to be alright…

At that exact moment, the door blew open to announce the arrival of a figure concealed underneath a thick winter jacket with the hood pulled up tight. She wrestled to close it on the breath of the storm, which had picked up quite significantly over a short amount of time. The barman polished a glass gleefully as the new visitor finally managed to shut out the rushing gale, which whistled irately in response to its denied entry.

This visitor disrobed the jacket in one graceful movement and hung it on one of the pegs by the fireplace as Maria watched from her seat at the corner, her eyes never leaving the figure who now made her way to the bar. She immediately recalled the texts from last night, which had ended in her inviting the subject of Dom's infidelity to meet in reception. And since the barman hadn't mentioned any other visitors, Maria reasoned that this simply had to be…Scarlett.

Maria could identify soft curves beneath a soaking wet red dress—the one she could have sworn that she once wore for Dom. As this stranger approached the barman, who continued to polish his glass, she tossed her drenched hair away from her face.

Although Maria had remarkably managed to prevent herself from falling apart, as soon as she noticed the deep flowing hair—which was no longer dark but now red—of the woman standing mere metres away, her heart was torn by frozen spears of ice. She knew exactly who this woman was, but how could this be?

This was not Scarlett…

…it was Carmilla.

## CHAPTER EIGHT

Before her sixteenth birthday, Carmilla recalled no purpose in life.

To celebrate this milestone age, she and a friend decided to hit one of the clubs in town as a fond farewell to one another. It was the summer holidays, and they were embarking on separate paths. Using her birthday money, Carmilla purchased her first grown-up dress. A red one which transfixed her. When they hit the town that night, all makeup and pushed-up cleavage, both were amazed by the attention they received. No longer subjected to the wolf whistles of acne-ridden teenagers or the gazes of adolescent boys during class. This was different—a taste of adulthood.

Carmilla was never comfortable being subjected to that kind of scrutiny, but after a few drinks, she began to unwind, her vision soon merging into a blur of bars, vomiting in the street and being refused entry from several clubs. The two girls eventually bumped into two men older than them by about ten years. They seemed fun initially. One of them couldn't take his eyes off Carmilla's red dress. Partially afflicted by the dulling of her inhibitions, Carmilla was somewhat intrigued by this handsome stranger with rugged features and a tailored grey suit. She giggled teasingly as he playfully remarked about his soft spot for that particular shade of red.

The other man brazenly leered at the girls, his sunken eyes emblazoned on a pallid, unhealthy complexion. He was much slimmer than his companion, with notably thinning hair, but dressed just as smartly, albeit in a much cheaper suit. Both girls fostered the opinion that he was a 'bit of a weirdo' as he fixed on them with a stagnant and uncomfortable, lingering stare.

Still, Carmilla was fascinated by the charm and confidence of the more attractive man and swiftly fell under his spell. After an argument with her friend, who suggested going home as she was tired, Carmilla found herself in the VIP area sipping champagne with her older escorts. She soon began to lose control of her faculties as the world stretched away from her…

…Carmilla estimated she was having a heart attack. Clutching her chest in the darkness, she could feel her pulse racing, causing her to feel giddy and light. As she lay there trying to contain herself, she saw movement in the gloom. Thick curtains forbid the glow of any streetlamp to penetrate the enclosure. Although the void appeared impenetrable, she sensed various shifting bodies of mass encircling her. She tried to assess the situation but could only manifest the vision of having drinks with two random guys she had met and leaving the pub as one held her up. How long ago that was, she had no way of knowing.

She panicked in response to heavy breathing somewhere between her legs but was now frozen and unable to move. Her thighs were forced open, and she noticed the figures becoming more excited. One frantically panted as another clambered on top of her and began thrusting slowly in and out. Her eyes pooled with tears, and now the figures were closer to her, frolicking inside her head. She was turned onto her front as warped faces flashed in and out of her awareness, and her unseen assailant groaned loudly.

Unable to move, for reasons unclear at the time, Carmilla had lain there for hours whilst one of them roughly sodomised her. The other stood at the foot of the bed, egging him on. The guy on top of her was talking to the spectator, a cacophony of words she couldn't fathom at first, but the last sentence was clear…

"Those who stare get nowhere."

The figure at the foot of the bed laughed whilst frantically stroking himself as the guy on top of her shuddered, and his orgasm filled her intestines.

During the ordeal, she must have passed out, only to awaken into consciousness as light tumbled in through gaps in the blinds. The room was spinning, and she had no grasp of how she had ended up in this unfamiliar bed. Initially, she allowed herself to pass everything off as a dream. It only took her a few moments to steady her swirling vision before the reality of the situation became clear. Beside her lay a naked figure, with his back to her, snoring without pause. She eased up off the bed, and a jolt of dizzying pain accompanied her movements.

She moved slowly so as not to disturb this unknown person, to realise that she, too, was also naked. A sharp spasm ran up her innards, and as she brought her hand to the source of the discomfort, a sheen of blood and fluid glazed over her fingers. Carmilla trembled as hysteria now began to assume control of her faculties. She left the bedroom behind her and saw she was in an apartment. The corridor ended with a doorway, which could only have been the front door. She entered the main living area and located her bag and red dress. Once she had dressed, she obeyed a compulsion to leave that place. After sneaking out of the front door, she ran and ran and ran down anomalous streets until her lungs burned. As she bent to take a breath, she felt the weight of her mobile phone in her bag. Quickly retrieving this, another jolt of panic consumed her as she realised it was well past midday, meaning Carmilla had no recollection of at least the last twelve hours. She resumed running through nameless streets in an unknown labyrinth of buildings, past knowing faces judging her as the world blurred.

In the subsequent days, Carmilla desperately tried

to piece together exactly what had happened. She tried contacting her friend, who wouldn't answer her call. Days became weeks, and Carmilla found herself disconnecting from the events, somehow blocking out much of the detail. It occurred to her that she simply couldn't bring herself to accept the truth and instead buried it, locking it away somewhere in her subconscious. And that's where the memory stayed...

...until she slept.

...because when Carmilla slept, those disjointed memories infested her dreams like a plague of locusts. Invading the void between dark and light as they cavorted and merged into faceless entities of her abuse. Each time, they grew in substance, manifesting into unclean pulsating apparitions until they were finally upon her, bound to her as insatiable Demons. Gleeful, wretched creatures, pleasuring themselves endlessly and adulterating her very essence with unrelenting malevolence.

As her spirit was crushed beneath this thrashing storm of unfolding madness, Carmilla lost hope.

Until finally...

...finally...

…The skies offered respite in the guise of an Angel, fashioned from a beam of light slicing through the storm…

…her Angel…

…Maria…

## CHAPTER NINE

At first, the two women merely stared at one another in silence. A cocktail of shock and surprise frolicked in the air between them, shaking and swirling as though charged with a hidden element.

Carmilla's pale skin flushed warmly against the flickering glow of flame. The licking shadows from the coal embers thrashed wildly at her as she crossed the carpet towards Maria, water running off her soaked clothing. Steam glazed over the moisture which clung to her as she neared.

Transfixed by her beauty, Maria ignored the situation in which she was entangled. Her fascination with Carmilla's inherent attraction and ability to draw people towards her, like she was gravity, now replaced by a potent but intoxicating level of jealousy—one she hadn't experienced before. As though reading her mind,

Carmilla licked her pronounced red lips and glided towards the table to take a seat. Crossing her leg, she exposed a long, slender thigh, which captivated Maria. Arousal now replaced any hatred for her unexpected love rival. A pair of red high-heeled shoes met the conclusion of Carmilla's long flowing legs. Maria's attention was arrested by a curious fleshy substance clinging to one of the heels.

The barman's gaze transfixed on Carmilla. He, too, was captivated by her beauty, his thoughts likely infused with all he would do to have her. Maria noticed the yearning dancing in his eyes and imagined he would probably crawl on his hands and knees over broken glass to get close to her. He certainly no longer smouldered with any sexual desire for Maria now that Carmilla had arrived.

Maria was seared with rage. Cast into the background again as a mere ghost to watch everyone else living their lives. Again, Maria was poisoned by a surge of envy. In Carmilla's presence, Maria seemed to no longer exist. For a fleeting moment, she realised she couldn't even recall her own name. It was like an unseen creature was burrowing away at her soul and somehow rewriting her memory.

Maria could see the barman's elation channelling into the fissures of his weathered face, no doubt imagining Carmilla's glistening wetness as he ran his tongue across his lips. Maria licked her lips in synchronicity, allowed herself to indulge in this shared yearning, and imagined what it must be like to have this effect on men.

*To be Carmilla.*

Maria recalled when Carmilla had suddenly just manifested into her life. They subsequently experimented with alcohol, drugs and, later on, one another. She didn't know much about Carmilla other than that she was a free spirit who was game for all but had a massive chip on her shoulder regarding men. Something had happened in her past that she got touchy with whenever Maria tried to pry. At the time, Maria tended to be more uptight and feared trying anything new. But Carmilla had entranced her. Her thick, flowing dark hair and pale, unblemished complexion. Her piercing blue eyes. Her long, slender legs. Despite being rough around the edges and harbouring a demeanour that betrayed a hidden trauma, she was the most attractive girl Maria had ever seen. Consequently, it didn't take long for her to fall under Carmilla's spell. At one point, she swore that she loved her. She was willing to give everything to her. Still, unexpectedly, Carmilla began to act distant towards Maria's deepening affection and vanished, breaking Maria's young heart. Their final moments together were spent beneath a blanket of rain as a storm approached, almost on such a night as this.

*Everyone leaves me in the end…*

Before long, Carmilla faded away from her entirely…until more recently, during that connection on the bridge…at the precise time Maria had considered ending it all…

"Carmilla… What the hell are you doing here?"

Carmilla's nose wrinkled at the sides, betraying a playful response to the enquiry.

"You already know, Maria… And please, call me Scarlett…if you prefer."

The words were remarkably enchanting, and Maria fell inside herself in a similar sensation to when she passed out earlier. It was as though she was gathering an awareness of the arrival of something she couldn't quite fathom, but not a thing of physical substance, more of a certainty. As though fate had wandered in from the storm, delivered to her in the form of her unexpected companion, who she now knew to be Dom's fling...*Scarlett*...but Maria did not harvest any judgment on behalf of her former lover. She felt calmer than ever before, as though each choice had led her to this singular occasion. As the gale picked up outside, whistling secrets against the window awning, Maria, in contrast, became oddly subdued, compliant within her surroundings and with a new perception of normality washing over her.

"But...how...why?"

Scarlett...*Carmilla*...ignored Maria whilst raising her arm and clicking her fingers in an audible snap. Within seconds, the barman was at her side like a loyal dog. Maria couldn't help but become drawn to a stirring which subtly stretched his trousers. Although this middle-aged pervert disgusted her, Maria couldn't remove herself from Carmilla's spell.

Carmilla ordered her new servant to go and lock the front door without drawing her attention from Maria. His brow furrowed, but the hypnotic quality of her voice caused him to obey her command. It was almost like the tone held a promise that it was in his best interests to do so. Much like Maria, he was helplessly passive to Carmilla's presence. With the clunk of the lock signalling no further interruption from the outside world, Carmilla finally turned to him, angling herself so he could see the pale flesh of her upper thigh.

"Now, why don't you be a good boy and get us a bottle of something nice…and two glasses."

Without a retort, the barman disappeared into a room behind the bar as Carmilla returned to Maria.

"Men…so predictable in their actions, and often, so wonderfully obedient when they think they have even a slight chance of getting their cock wet. Clay for us to play with and mould into our fantasies."

The barman arrived with a bottle of expensive-looking red wine, placed the glasses on the table between Maria and Carmilla, and began working the corkscrew into the stem. His forehead glazed with moisture in response to his efforts, and Maria could smell a hint of musk from his sweat.

Carmilla continued her speech, "Men can pretend to be in control all they wish, but really, we command the strength; we hold the power. Isn't that right?"

Carmilla reached up to the barman, who was struggling with the corkscrew, and she placed a pale, slender hand on his chest. Blood rushed to the surface of his heavily wrinkled face—an unkind face that now betrayed a sneer of disdain.

"Anything you say, lady."

Finally, the cork was free of the bottle, and the barman began filling the glasses on the table, excitement etched in the contours of his worn skin.

All Maria could do was watch. She was transfixed and unexpectedly aroused by the strangeness of this interaction and convinced that she was frozen in a dream. Yet, could dreams feel this vivid?

Carmilla gestured for the barman to pass her the bottle, which he did gently before taking a seat between the two ex-lovers and raising his glass awkwardly, attempting to toast. Ignoring his futile gesture, Carmilla's expression blazed with menacing intent.

"But those all too eager to obey…bore me to death…"

Carmilla swung the bottle at the barman's temple just as the glass met his lips, resulting in an explosion of crystal shards which tore across his flesh. A fountain of blood and teeth sprayed the air as the barman slumped to the floor, clutching wildly at his face.

Carmilla moved quickly, directly positioning her heel above his head as he twisted and turned in agony. Maria froze, not in reflex to the violence but to the utterance that floated towards her in slow motion—the exact words on the ceiling back at the lodge.

"Those who stare get nowhere."

Carmilla's heel disappeared into the barman's orbital bone with a sickening crunch. Although Maria couldn't help but marvel at the precision of the violence, her stomach spasmed in response to the garbled squealing from the barman, whose legs now started to kick and flail as he screamed in an unnaturally warped high pitch.

Carmilla extracted her foot with a sucking sound and drove her heel meticulously into his other socket. His muscles abruptly contorted in one last effort. Silence began to consume the bar, and the tempest outside seemed to take a breath. Carmilla's silhouette cast a long shadow from the fireplace over the barman as his pulsing body finally stilled.

"I can always see it in their eyes, and this one is the worst calibre. One who has convinced himself that his actions are justified, without anyone judging his thoughts. A pathetic complacency which allows him to indulge in his sexual gratification. I do not doubt that you or I would have been the subject of his masturbation later tonight...had I not acted accordingly."

Maria could not remove her gaze from the barman. Ichorous fluid drained out of his misshapen orbital cavities, but his chest did not rise and fall. Maria felt the world around her stretching away, as though in exhalation, which altered her perception and detached her from the situation.

"Their eyes betray their real underlying motive, and this fool here had it coming!"

Carmilla glanced down at her metallic heel and giggled at the sinewy remnant of one of the barman's eyes. She surveyed it in amazement, then carefully withdrew the bloodied orb and placed it on the table near Maria, who remained present, but disconnected from the madness. Hadn't she considered removing the barman's eyes right before Carmilla swept in?

"Men like him are common, and I have no interest in indulging them. There is little to gain. He will now carry the gift of blindness on his travels and have eternity to fine-tune his remaining senses...and he will need it."

Maria noticed an intense rush filling the coils of her abdomen, and a surging, violent convulsing caused her to vomit over the table and floor, the recent spectacle too much for her to physically comprehend. After expelling all she could, Maria rose out of her chair, intent on vacating the situation. Her legs buckled under her weight, and she helplessly crashed back onto her chair as Carmilla returned to the seat across from her.

The smile tearing across Carmilla's face concerned Maria more than the corpse at her feet. It was a monstrous sneer that contained no warmth behind it. With absolute and petrifying certainty, Maria surmised that Carmilla was not the same girl she knew all those years ago.

## CHAPTER TEN

"I have missed you, Maria."

Carmilla still wore the malevolent grin from earlier, but her demeanour carried a more reassuring expression, encouraging Maria to believe the sincerity of her words.

Maria had so many questions and didn't know where to start. There was a dead fucking person, with destroyed eyes, lying on the floor beside them, something which didn't seem to bother Carmilla in the slightest. Not to mention Dom's savagely disfigured body back at the lodge. Running on adrenaline, Maria engaged the elephant in the room.

"Carmilla...what have you done?"

Carmilla allowed her smile to drop briefly before rolling her eyes at the deceased barman.

"I am trying to have a fucking conversation here,

and you are on about this fucking closet masturbater here? I told you, I can see it in their eyes, right? Especially this one…"

The unkind smirk reappeared, causing a considerable shiver to flicker along the tiny hairs on Maria's spine. Outside, the wind whistled and swooshed through the cabin's wooden joists, screaming an ushered warning that Maria could not yet translate.

A vision flashed within Maria's consciousness of Dom, back in the cabin, lying there with his cock torn off…his eyes brutally destroyed, just like the barman.

*Those who stare get nowhere…*

Carmilla's pupils enlarged as though in response to these unsaid echoes, and a shudder of electricity slivered across her scalp.

"Why don't you ask me the real question on your mind, Maria?"

The menace drained from Carmilla's face, and her beauty returned. Her soft pale cheeks, unwrinkled skin and thick red hair painted a picture of innocence encircling her demeanour.

"Did you kill Dom…Dominic?"

Carmilla stood up instead of answering and

turned away, pacing to the window as she spoke.

"Dominic was…special. Don't you remember telling me that when I embraced you? After I took you in from the cold? You do remember he left you out in the cold, right?"

Now, by the aperture, Carmilla breathed on the glass and used her finger to draw a love heart in the mist.

"Carmilla, did you kill him?"

Despite presuming it to be the more logical conclusion, Maria needed to hear it from Carmilla.

"All in good time, Maria. But first, I want you to tell me exactly how much you know about Dominic. Not much, I bet?"

Maria felt a chill quivering in her stomach, spreading quickly to her chest. This was an excellent point…she didn't know much about Dominic. He enjoyed going out with his friends, playing poker, watching football, and whatever else they got up to in town. Other than his fascination for anal sex and that he was a sucker for red underwear, what did she really know?

Carmilla fixed deeply into Maria's soul with a

scrutiny that Maria could only describe as menacing. A projection of understanding gradually glazed over Carmilla as she translated Maria's abject look of confusion as sincere, and the words remaining unsaid were slowly beginning to have an effect.

Maria had to focus hard to follow her thoughts back to the night she and Dominic had argued, and he had left her out on the street—the fractured vision of reconnecting with Carmilla.

Was it just a coincidence that Carmilla had arrived at that exact moment?

Dominic then accused Maria of betraying him, leading to the subsequent downfall of their relationship. Although it had seemed like a dream at the time, which she blamed on a combination of argument, cold air, and alcohol, Carmilla's presence confirmed the memory as sincere.

Carmilla shifted her gaze away from Maria and to the storm outside. "Men like Dominic just love to play the victim. It helps them justify their choices. They assume no responsibility for their actions. They reflect their behaviour on the victims of their wrongdoings."

Carmilla drew a cross over the love heart on the

misted window and spun to face Maria.

"How did you meet Dominic, Carmilla?" Maria was unsure if she really wanted to know the answer, but the mark of deceit bestowed upon her strengthened her resolve. If Dominic had indeed been a cheating bastard, and that much was becoming quite clear, then he deserved what had happened to him. But what about Carmilla, her friend, and her ex-lover?

*How could she?*

Maybe she would lure this bitch back to the cabin and drown her in that fucking tub. Or perhaps if she had just drowned herself earlier, she wouldn't have to deal with this shit.

Carmilla ignored the enquiry, evidently in her own world, with her own agenda, and headed to the bar, collecting a bottle of malt and two tumblers. She placed them on the table and sat across from Maria, studying her intently.

"All in good time. Now, you will need something more substantial to drink. Why don't you fill those tumblers, and I will share my story with you?"

Maria hated whiskey but craved something to take the edge off her altered perception of things. She surveyed Carmilla, comparing her perfect appearance with her own. Even with soaked hair and no makeup, she was insanely hot.

*Why couldn't she be more like Carmilla?*

Maria removed the bottle top with an unexpectedly steady hand and poured two large measures of the smoky, golden liquid. The smell of spicy, woody notes lifted as the walls closed around Carmilla, deforming her silhouette. After a sip of her malt, Carmilla relaxed back into the chair, and as the embers in the fire behind her cracked and spit, she spoke in a calm, resolute tone…

\*

Maria drew her gaze over the brutally distorted profile of the barman on the floor as her thoughts flooded with Carmilla's words. Revelations of the assault echoed within her, sending her senses into overdrive. She felt pity for Carmilla. But was this enough to justify her recent actions?

Something began to stir amongst the thrashing waves of Maria's subconscious—a manifestation of escalating whispers that swam the unexplored depths of her, carrying a message yet indecipherable. Maria perceived the air to be thickening and an unseen crushing weight exerting itself on her chest. She could feel a fiery irritation swelling in her intestines, and a potent acrid film lined her saliva.

Carmilla grinned wildly at the understanding now projecting from Maria's demeanour and spoke with an excited undertone to her words…words which lit up as vivid pictures in Maria's mind, almost as if the memory was somehow hers…

"…Remember how I used to find it hard to sleep, Maria?"

Maria's psyche was ablaze with fractured memories of Dominic, Carmilla's red dress…*her* red dress. The confusion began to eat away at a clarity that had started unfolding. Carmilla's story was unsettlingly familiar, and a creeping sense of unease latched onto her nerve. Carmilla's voice was hypnotic, like white noise massaging into Maria's anxiety. Her head became uncomfortably heavy, but she felt compelled to answer Carmilla's question with a yawn.

"Of course I do…"

"Did my story bore you, Maria?"

Maria's eyes glazed over. A cocktail of shock and whiskey presumably numbed her perception. As though tuning out from her surroundings, the atmosphere began swimming and dancing as her current awareness and imagination twisted into a kaleidoscope of fragmented images.

"How do you sleep at night, Maria? You wear those dark rings under your eyes like a badge of honour."

"No…I…sometimes…not much recently…"

"You slept well last night, though, didn't you, my angel? Something you drank, maybe?"

The mention of the champagne at the lodge caused a knot to formulate in Maria's stomach. She recalled how greedily Dominic had devoured both drinks and how deeply he had slept, then how she had passed out into oblivion afterwards. But how on earth had Scarlett…had Carmilla?

"You look tired, Maria… Close your eyes, I have a secret to share with you…"

Maria relaxed her breathing further until she was a slave to the heavying drapes of her eyelids, and the soft embrace of shadows carried her off to sleep.

"Come with me...just follow my voice..."

*...into the darkness...*

## CHAPTER ELEVEN

*…into the darkness…*

*It was the shuffling that she noticed first…*

*Warmth covered her skin like a blanket of glowing embers. The heat intensified, which did little to comfort her from the approaching sound of something sizable scuttling along the floor nearby. Her eyes fixed open, and immediately, whatever came towards her gave pause.*

*Glancing around, it took a second or two for her to determine her surroundings. It became clear that she was now back in the cabin and on top of the bed. Her mind quickly retreated to when she had awoken to discover what was left of Dominic and, later, of the brutality Carmilla had inflicted on the barman. How long ago those events had occurred, or even if the whole thing had been a bad dream, she could not tell. A cold shiver crept over her spine as the scuttling noise from earlier returned. Something stirred in the hallway, and it did so with purpose. The scraping and shuffling ended momentarily as whatever it was reached the closed door with a wet thump.*

*Somewhere outside of the cabin window, Maria could sense another presence attempting to tear into existence. Tentacles worming out from its sightless voids. Attracted to her fruitless endeavours to decipher the unfolding madness.*

*The bedroom door vibrated in response to what Maria could only imagine as fingernails clawing frantically over wood, and a splintering and wretched weeping began to shred away at her nerve.*

*She could not move but to train her attention on the door, which acted as a temporary barrier to whatever lurked beyond it, squirming and groaning. The handle turned, but the other side's efforts were hindered, as though whatever sought entry to the room didn't have the use of human faculties.*

*A flash of a memory, of a naked figure lying on a bed with terrible injuries, oscillated through her awareness. The image struck disgust in her but also fear.*

*She was just about to yell when the truth of whatever tried to burrow its way into the room with her was revealed. The latch dropped, and the door swung steadily ajar.*

*Initially, she would have sworn that the organism twisting and shuddering on the floor was a giant pulsating arachnid. But did arachnids have torn flesh covered in a glaze of scarlet? Did they have only four awkwardly arranged legs? Could they utter a groan as petrifying as this wretched abomination?*

*What Maria looked at could barely be certified as anything but a monster. It crawled clumsily on four terribly warped limbs, amazingly holding the body aloft. From what she could gather, this atrocity resembled a chaotic assembly of misshapen human flesh. A ragged gaping hole twitched between its two front appendages, which she understood to be its legs. She discerned an object swinging like a pendulum at its rear as it approached. The grotesque creature turned clumsily, and Maria's heart bellowed in her ears as the room walls spasmed and cracked as though animated by the excitement of this spectacle.*

*Was it possible for nightmares to be so vivid?*

*A terribly deformed neck barely managed to carry the head, which swung down unnaturally from side to side. It frantically contorted to expose cavernous eyeholes, which gazed at her, unseeing but tuned in to her presence. A tortured cry oozed from its wretched mouth. The sound was petrifying and sent a jolt of electricity through Maria, causing her to try and shake herself free of this horror, but she could not move. When she tried to scream, her vocal cords refused to produce any sound.*

*Although only a portion of its characteristics could be identified as human, the certainty of what now stood before her on hideously contoured flesh was unmistakable. This beast of sinew and bone and brutal injury was Dominic. The man she once loved was now crafted into an impossibly fashioned monstrosity. Shadows stretched from the corners of the room, manipulating the darkness to become gleeful, wretched guardians mustering around Dominic's pitiful ensemble of limbs and holes.*

*From the tortured miscreation which desperately reached up to her, a disfigured mouth tore open and spoke in a gargled, spluttering warble.*

*"Maria...please...help me!"*

\*

Maria opened her eyes, but the morbidly vivid nightmare lingered on her nerves. As consciousness flowed in aggressively with a searing headache, she realised she was back in bed. A jolt of electricity crawled along her skin. Had the entire thing been a dream? Was she dreaming now? The reverberation from nearby told her otherwise.

"Welcome back to the land of the living."

Carmillas's tone was ominous, hypnotic.

"Not much of a whiskey drinker...huh...I will remember that. You really passed out, didn't you? You went out like a light! So I decided to bring you back to the lodge... What are friends for, eh?"

Maria had many questions, but for now, she had a compulsion to breathe and escape this madness. Hell, she would die for a dip in that fucking hot tub whilst looking up at the stars, anything but that nightmare *(is that what it was?)*. She smiled in remorseful understanding that her mind was indeed lost and her thoughts corrupted by the insanity which now consumed every waking moment. But at least she was no longer alone when darkness came for her.

*Just what the fucking fuck was that dream?*

Closing her eyelids tightly, she prayed that all this was indeed a dream. Still, amongst the gloom, the shadows contorted and twisted into the shape of a creature, horribly deformed on all fours, furiously clutching at her... *Maria...please...help me...*

"Maria?"

In response to Carmilla's gentle utterance, Maria reopened her eyes and immediately tuned in to her surroundings. Although her flesh felt numb, her senses were now amplified. A subtle earthy smell entered her nose and throat, and she imagined the storm filling her lungs with each breath. Her physical being seemed to become one with the elements, and a coppery bitter taste glazed her tongue. This sensation intensified as she visualised the spilling of blood from two caverns on the barman's face and of Dominic's messed up body as it crawled its way towards her, the dream stubbornly lingering within her. Goosebumps rose excitedly towards a potent force binding onto her.

"Carmilla...what the hell is going on?"

"Shhhhh...Maria. I need you to remain strong for this next part. With great power comes great responsibility and all that shit..."

Carmilla laughed triumphantly as she gently placed her cold palm against Maria's cheek.

"What did you see when you closed your eyes?"

Maria pushed Carmilla's hand away, and Carmilla beamed playfully whilst Maria eased herself up off the bed. Her head was splitting, and she was in no mood for games anymore. A distinctive certainty gathering in the atmosphere now translated into a compulsion for

Maria not to inform Carmilla about the man she loved dragging himself along the recesses of her brain. Or about the shameless, writhing horrors accompanying him, tearing away his meat and pervading his orifices with glistening and dripping malice. She almost chuckled at seeing him, helpless to their frenzied attack. Maybe if she could keep him locked away in her labyrinth, she would grow to relish observing his helpless form reaching out to her. To him, she would be a god; to her, he would be…a pet.

Maria wondered how long it would take before Dominic learned the fissures and routes within her.

"Please tell me, my angel, was Dominic there? You were calling out his name as you slept."

A momentary flicker that ran over Carmilla's pupils betrayed a secret motive amongst her confidence. Maria's mind kindled to the promise of clandestine knowledge, which Carmilla's demeanour teased her with. Despite the severity of the situation, Maria noticed her posture steeling itself in response. As though invaded by an unseen force, a formidable motivation now crept inside her. She must assert control to avoid facing the wrath of whatever Carmilla had in store.

"Dominic is fucking dead...Carmilla...you *fucking* killed him!"

Maria's voice carried an unfamiliar menace, and she enjoyed its effect on Carmilla's disposition as she softened her features and stepped away from the bed.

"Yet, you were calling out his name. Did he reach out to you from the darkness? Damn...he must have actually loved you in his own fucked up way if he is seeking you out from beyond the grave." Carmilla pondered this notion.

Still sluggish from passing out, Maria's thoughts began to formulate into a confirmation that she must indeed be suffering from psychological trauma...at the very least...

...she barely felt alive anymore.

Something hidden compelled her to translate the peculiar riddle that had danced out of the storm to connect with the fissures of her physical being.

Maria got to her feet, but a torrent of blood rushing to her temple caused her to lose balance, and she stumbled forward. Carmilla steadied her on the shoulder, but Maria shrugged her off and staggered out into the hallway.

Flashes of that creature on all fours from her nightmare *(was that a nightmare?)* flooded her vision, enticing her to check on Dominic in the other room. Could he really be that hideous abomination? She hesitated briefly, then opened the door as Carmilla loomed behind her.

Maria's world folded in on itself as she gathered the composure to meet the blank gaze of Dominic's lifeless face, which was now drained of any colour. Although deathly still, the position of his body was comparable to that monster from her nightmare, the image of which haunted her. A vivid tapestry of adulterated flesh fashioned by the brutally disfigured corpse of Dominic. His unnaturally twisted neck, vacant eyeholes, and awkwardly contorted limbs crawling stealthily from the deepest recesses of her subconscious as though a spider seeking its prey.

A surge of lightheadedness took Maria, and she covered her mouth as a scalding hot rush of whiskey-tasting vomit raced into her throat. She made it to the toilet just in time for the contents of her stomach to spray thickly into the cistern. The bitter, smoky tang of whiskey ran over her tongue, joined with the metallic hint of blood, and Maria cried out at the overwhelming potency of the flavours.

Carmilla stood beneath the doorway, disgust carved across her face, until Maria eventually flushed the toilet and barged past Carmilla into the kitchen to gulp several cups of water.

Carmilla appeared again at the doorway, now with a frustrated demeanour. "Are we quite finished?"

Another flash from that dream, of something watching her from outside of the window. Maria dropped the empty cup in the sink and hurried to the bedroom. Gazing out through the misted window, she met only her own blurred silhouette, any features now distorted by the rain.

Shaking the dream away, Maria returned to Carmilla and sat at the kitchen table. In contrast to the cabin, which swayed and eased under the pressure of the unrelenting rain and wind, Maria became poised and unmoving, which seemed to unsettle Carmilla.

"Okay, Carmilla. No more fucking bullshit! Tell me what the fuck is going on?"

## CHAPTER TWELVE

Rain pounded an aggressive symphony on the top of the cabin in sheets, like countless spears frantically eager to puncture the outer shell. The foul weather appeared to have taken out many of the surrounding lights in the area. Within the cabin, the luminescent glow from the downlights illuminated Maria and Carmilla as they faced one another over the table. Maria's skin took on an unnatural shade of green, her eyes red and tired. She could taste bile in her throat, which rose into her mouth as Carmilla spoke.

"I have always loved the rain. When I was younger, as my friends ran home to seek refuge, I would remain outside and allow it to cleanse me. Nature's own therapy soaking away my anxieties. My parents would go crazy at this when I arrived home, soaked through. They told me I wasn't normal. But I couldn't get enough of it."

Maria's body warmed under the consuming spell of Carmilla's words. Both girls fell silent as a rumble of thunder shook the sky. As though in response, the rain tapped more frantically. The smell of the storm filled the air, a sweet, earthy fragrance which seemed to amplify with Carmilla's words.

"Remember that night when you joined me outside in the rain?"

Maria was unsure whether she had already pondered the memory or whether Carmilla's voice triggered the vivid image. It curiously felt as if the recollection was shared by them both. She could sense the positivity returned in Carmilla's softening demeanour as a warm tingle crawled over her scalp, and the memory unfolded...

*...On that particular night, they were both eighteen. After a drunken evening, Maria had awoken to find Carmilla sitting alone on the balcony, crying, under a heavy downpour. Carmilla turned to face her with eyes worn red from sorrow. Maria responded by joining her and taking her hand. The sensation was overwhelming to Maria at first. Still, as she watched Carmilla let go of her tears and eventually relax in answer to the relentless*

*burrowing raindrops, she allowed herself to try to let go of her own anxieties. After a few moments, she could hardly notice the rain, just a million fingers massaging them gently, removing all their stresses, as they sat cojoined beneath the onslaught.*

Carmilla's voice manifested like a hypnotic rhythm dancing in the air, replacing the memory and somehow in synchronicity with the melody carried by the rain.

"I almost told you my secret on the balcony, but I didn't want to crush you with the truth. That's why I decided it was best to leave you. You didn't deserve my problems, but now…now you can say we are connected."

Maria's stomach tightened with excitement and fear at whatever Carmilla would bestow upon her. She reached across the table and took her hands in a false show of companionship. Even with her issues, Carmilla was much more alluring than Maria, but she didn't seem to value any of this.

Carmilla's skin was bathed pale, but her irises flickered excitedly as lightning filled the world outside. Maria stole from Carmilla's disposition that she would soon be made privy to a truly special phenomenon. Her hair tingled as Carmilla finally began to unload her burden.

"...After I was...attacked, I started drinking a lot. I found myself sucked into a black hole whilst a forbidden craving within me clutched back at the scraps of reality to take control. To disarm this sickness, I allowed myself to sink into a meaningless void. Being off my head on drugs or alcohol took the edge off initially, but it wasn't sustainable, so I sunk deeper. Next, I indulged in the company of men. I went from one fucking asshole to another, experimenting with all sorts of debauchery. In a peculiar twist of fate, sex with a faceless kaleidoscope of countless men balanced my fractured mind. The more I yielded to my urges, the further away from hell I travelled. Attracting men who are only after one thing is quite simple. Mere lambs to sacrifice to my...needs. Each sexual encounter granted me respite from my demons, much more than drugs and alcohol, and I couldn't snap out of the routine. It became a necessary evil. My fix! I enjoyed their little games as time passed, and I even noticed the patterns in their behaviour. Enough to lead them along longer than they initially planned. I made the game my own and used it to keep my demons at bay. But they were waiting and watching. They only struck when I was alone, as soon as the quiet crept in to feed on me."

Maria allowed herself to sink into Carmilla's recollection, noticing a more profound connection. It seemed bizarre that a sense of déjà vu clung to each sentence Carmilla spoke.

"Whenever I closed my eyes, they would come. Leading the group was always the same anonymous fucking *cunt*. At the start, I must have blanked out his features, my mind conjuring the experience into a weird Frankenstein's monster of what they did to me."

Carmilla looked at peace as she spoke. It was as if the revelations she had finally shared began to manifest into something genuinely believable. About those nightmares which taunted her since that assault on her flesh. About creatures reaching out to her from the darkness. Countless sexually motivated apparitions, fighting among themselves, all keen to have their way with her…

"…Projections of my suppressed anxieties…a parasite, crafted by my actions. Bred from my…." Carmilla motioned wildly with both hands at her temples, her eyes pooled with tears, and her bottom lip trembling. She gazed vacantly out the window at the howling storm as the catalyst for her compulsive behaviour ran itself over her memories. These revelations scratched into the foundations of Maria's existence like blades, inviting unseen parasitic worms through the fresh fissures which began to feast on her consciousness.

"And then I met...you, my angel. You replaced the rain and the darkness. You gave me hope. But as the tendrils of your love tightened themselves around me, they caused those demons to stir. The more I tried to ignore them, the stronger they returned, until I even felt their terrible eyes upon me when I was awake. They were constantly fucking there. I couldn't sleep and prayed for the rain and when we would be together because I am free only under those raindrops or with you."

Maria reflected on the rare occasions she could recall Carmilla falling asleep. Much of their time was spent awake until dawn. On one of those nights, Carmilla shared her rage towards men. Maria knew Carmilla had much more bubbling underneath the surface but chose not to pry. Carmilla tried to blame her hatred of men on her preference for female flesh, and Maria had held her tightly, assuring her that as long as they had each other, the past could be relinquished…

*…Maria awoke one evening to Carmilla's cries in the dark. She was sweating after quite a severe nightmare, and Maria immediately went to her side. She was concerned by the level of terror and helplessness in Carmilla's dull expression. Eyes etched with a fragility she hadn't seen in anyone before. But glistening within her pupils, her reflection cast back at her of someone less than Carmilla.*

The previous notion of jealousy, which had poisoned Maria, now evolved into an abject disgust for Carmilla. No matter what she fucking did, she had company. Even the figments of her imagination were obsessed with her… and she didn't appreciate it. She didn't know what it was like to feel alone…especially in the darkness. But Carmilla was unloading on her, finally, and the more she did, the more Maria felt in…control. She decided to retain her composure.

"Carmilla…why didn't you tell me? Back then? You needed help! I could have helped…"

"I thought about it… I thought about it for a

while, and I was so close to sharing everything with you, but you used to look at me with so much love, and I never wanted that to change. So I decided that night in the rain that I had to escape...

"...Our final time together on that balcony...in the rain...that memory has been the only thing offering me a beacon of hope to keep me going, even in the lowest moments which followed. I always held on to a strand of hope that we would face the monsters together one day. And here we are...united by fate."

Maria mentally replayed the encounter on the balcony in the rain, when she had just declared her love for Carmilla and Carmilla, in turn, had seriously lost control. Screaming at her, *"You don't really fucking know me."* However, Maria now knew her feelings to have been nothing more than an infatuation for Carmilla's often overbearing confidence. A figurehead that men and women flocked to without much effort on her behalf, just as she had...

Maria's adolescent heart had been broken, and she had never held much worth for herself since then. Carmilla's presence may have even been the catalyst for Maria's subsequent lack of confidence and her disconnection from who she truly was.

Despite now being aware of the figments of Carmilla's nightmares and about the men who had had their way with her, Maria couldn't help but feel a hatred towards her. Maria was so used to being alone in the dark. But Carmilla…

…Carmilla did not cherish her etched memories, now bathed in shadows. She simply took it all for granted!

Maria fixed her gaze on Carmilla and hoped that her demeanour portrayed a feeling of pity rather than the burning resentment she now carried. It was beginning to make sense why Carmilla distrusted men when they met, why she couldn't sleep, but why was she sharing this now?

"But why are you telling me all this now, Carmilla?"

Carmilla clung to Maria's wrists desperately as she spoke. "Because now, we are connected. And now we can rid ourselves of these monsters, Maria, of all who wronged us. Together. Memories of those wrongs are cast into our subconscious like a disease. They infest us. Like that bastard Dominic…the disgusting barman!"

"I understand why you killed that barman, Carmilla, really I do. But did you honestly kill Dominic just for me?"

Carmilla's complexion transformed, her skin filling with blood until she blazed ember red, and a flicker of madness shifted over her eyes. This transformation intimidated Maria, who dropped her shoulders until Carmilla continued.

"Not just for you, Maria. I killed Dominic for *us*. He may just have cheated on you, but he did so much worse to me…"

Maria returned to the dream about Dominic, which at the moment offered a much more tolerable reality than here.

"After I left you, I relapsed to my old ways. It was the only outlet I understood to assert dominance. But the light you cast into my soul would eventually allow me to regain strength. It took me a few years to give up on using drugs and meaningless sex to keep my demons at bay. I genuinely thought I was winning the battle, but the more sober I was…the more alone I was…until they reappeared stronger. Their features manifested from faceless apparitions to creatures with more substance. To human faces, which began to haunt my waking life. My memories twisted into one continuous kaleidoscope of unrelenting chaos. One night, during heavy rainfall, which I could always rely on, they infiltrated my psyche, tethered somehow to the storm. With the final barrier now down, they were free to have me at any time, and that's when my world fell apart. I started walking. I wasn't sure where I was going, but impulse drew me forward. I even considered throwing myself off a bridge to finish it all. But I kept walking. The rain continued long into the evening, and I found myself on the streets we used to walk together…and when the rain finally eased off, I saw one of my monsters in the flesh…"

## CHAPTER THIRTEEN

*Carmilla pulled her jacket up closer around her neck and allowed her breath to mist in the air as cars passed in a blur between her and the row of pubs across the road.*

*As the Saturday afternoon hordes of shoppers, drinkers, and wanderers busied along, she crossed the road and stopped outside a bar she had once frequented. The window reflected someone else entirely—an unremarkable silhouette of a forgettable revenant. Sunken eyes cast into dark rings in her colourless face were her only distinguishing characteristic. Her reflection distorted, merging with the bustling punters beyond…and she finally saw…him.*

*His stillness in the crowd had attracted Carmilla's attention, overwhelming her with the familiarity of his demeanour. He was poised amongst his companions like a wolf in sheep's clothing, with his white fitted shirt stretching tight over his muscular shoulders and tapered blue jeans. However, his perfect, gentlemanly manner betrayed all Carmilla knew him to be, and as her heart rose to her throat, a seed of doubt infected her.*

*Carmilla had to be clear that this was him…*

*After entering the bar, Carmilla sat near the group to confirm her attacker's identity. After a few moments, there was no doubt. It wasn't the hidden motive behind his smile or his perfectly styled spiky hair and lightly tanned skin. It was something about his aura. His presence…*

*…her monster.*

*Carmilla's stomach knotted and began to crawl, repulsed that at least one of the bastards in this happy-go-lucky bunch was a fucking rapist.*

*The friends looked to be in high spirits, and from what Carmilla could gather, they were celebrating the win of a football team they supported. Carmilla watched as the beer flowed and the younger members blatantly ogled over the girls. At the same time, her monster remained stalwart and measured at the centre of the small huddle, seemingly unaffected by the sins of his past, cocooned in his own agenda. Carmilla wondered if his ruminations carried a memory of her, and a slither of electricity danced over her flesh.*

*As though sensing her intrusion into his thoughts, he even glanced at Carmilla. He sneered and invited a friend to observe this gaunt and worn woman soaked to the skin—a woman he had drugged and abused several years earlier.*

*Enraged but relieved that he didn't recognise her, she turned away to notice a girl in a red dress sweeping into the bar. An outfit not too dissimilar to the one she had on when she was raped. Carmilla perceived the atmosphere stretching away from her and tuning in to her heartbeat as it shuddered and boomed in her ears.*

*She knew this girl in red and nearly ran to her before she realised her body had frozen. Could it really be her?*

*…but she only had eyes for one person.*

*Carmilla spun away from her to see…him…*

*It was like a moment of déjà vu. Carmilla would have sworn she was dreaming had she not stepped aside to witness her friend Maria wrapping her arms around…Dominic…*

"…I felt what I can only describe as madness and left the bar to hyperventilate outside. The scene beyond the window proved the sincerity of what I was witnessing. It was you…and him…"

Maria now struggled to recollect that night—when she and Dominic had had that argument…

…he left her out in the cold…

…she had walked to the outskirts of town and considered ending it all.

"I followed you that night, my angel, always keeping out of sight. I initially assumed you might have been involved with what happened to me. Still, I accepted this as a morbid coincidence. I saw you and Dominic arguing, then getting into a taxi. I worried I had lost my chance to warn you—to save you. I panicked and spent the next hour walking the streets. I was about to give up until I saw you on that bridge."

Maria could recall Carmilla's arrival but couldn't remember much about the rest of that evening. It was mostly a blur, concluding with her awakening to the buzzer and Dominic. As if her memories were being consumed by an unseen parasitic worm.

"When Dom screwed you last night, he probably did so while imagining me. I wouldn't be surprised if his friend, Justin, spectated. You see when we reconnected on the bridge, you told me through drunken tears all about Dominic. About your plans for the future. About what makes him tick, and of course, about this little romantic break you had planned. Your demeanour was all wrong, however. You were incomplete, but you did have fire in you. You probably won't remember telling me that you would cut his dick off had he cheated and fed it to him, and about his anal sex fixation, something we both know about... as does he now..."

A flash of Dominic brutally disfigured translated from Carmilla's words into a vivid picture within Maria's mind.

"You inspired my subsequent course of action. In your presence, with my motivation to exact vengeance on Dominic, the creatures shrunk back into the hell they had spawned from. But this time would be different. This time, our connection was much more profound. I decided to track Dominic down. This would allow me to test out his love for you and give him the chance to recognise me. I was entitled to have a lot of fun and enjoy myself after the past few years. So, I gave myself a little makeover...

...and Scarlett was born..."

## CHAPTER FOURTEEN

The person across the table from Maria no longer seemed weary of the burdens inflicted by the past. Her eyes no longer lacked life; instead, they burned with intent. Carmilla was a butterfly that had shed its skin from the caterpillar's shrivelling carcass.

    The revelations of Carmilla's story reverberated along Maria's nerves in synchronisation with the storm. It was almost as though, with Carmilla's metamorphosis unfolding before her, Maria was also going through her own significant change. Where it would lead her, she did not yet know. What did occur to her was an overwhelming sense of poised rage, which currently bubbled beneath the surface of her exterior. She didn't think it wise to share this with Carmilla. As Carmilla had kept her secrets from Maria for so long, she was entitled to her surreptitious thoughts.

Only yesterday, she had been blissfully ignorant of Dominic's past. Also, she had cast Carmilla into the shadows of her past. She was dealing with her problems whilst finding a way to creep forward and carve her own trajectory. All until Carmilla came back in and disrupted her foundations. If it weren't for this beautiful person sitting across from her, a person scarred with the past, Maria wouldn't be faced with the horror which unfolded. Could she really put all of this behind her and move forward with Carmilla?

Carmilla's face lit up against a flash of lightning. The thunder was booming closely, its wrath now entirely upon Lakeside Cabins, its aftermath yet to be determined. Her story approached a conclusion that Maria already knew as if she was the one reliving the memory.

"I chose my red dress and found *suitable* shoes for the occasion. You told me that Dominic couldn't resist a woman in red, so I changed my hair. Do you like it?"

Carmilla's red hair suited her perfectly. And it pissed Maria off. How could someone dragged out of the grave change their appearance overnight?

"Dominic avoided me all night. Unlike the other

boys in the bar, he didn't acknowledge me. He didn't seem interested in me, and that pissed me off. At one point, I even began to question my worth. Not many men have that effect on me, but it intoxicates me on the rare occasion it happens…drives me crazy…"

Carmilla's eyes dulled as she retold her account of meeting Dominic.

"…after a few hours, we stood side by side in the bar, and he didn't even grant me a courtesy ogle…I mean, look at me, right?"

Ignoring for a moment the insanity of the situation, Maria observed Scarlett standing by the window. Although slender, she had curves. Her new red hair draped over her shoulders, the tips like flames licking to reach her prominent yet modest cleavage. One thing was sure amid all of this madness. She was fucking hot as hell.

In contrast to her own decidedly average form, once again, Maria felt a surge of jealousy, much more potent now…and something else…stirring within that mixture of feelings—a certainty yet to manifest fully in the seas of her awareness.

"This version of Dominic undeniably piqued my

interest. He didn't appear bound by the same impulses as his friends, who couldn't keep their eyes off me. Finally, though, I managed to attract his attention by brushing past him at the bar. I expected him to be dumbfounded by my beauty; at the very least, I wanted him to recognise me, but he continued his game nonetheless."

Maria's rage now attained fever pitch as she thought of Dominic, that cheating fucking bastard, and not just Dominic, but her fucking friend, both of the fucking bastards...but then why was Carmilla's recollection almost the same as her own with Dominic, when they first met? Carmilla held Maria's gaze as she recited Dominic's words, and a spear of ice pierced Maria's heart; it was the exact line he had used on her.

*"Your shoes look really comfortable..."*

Carmilla bent one knee to show off her exceptionally high-heeled shoes, which remained glazed in sinew and blood.

"A stupid fucking line that only a bunch of stupid fucking women would fall for. Stupid fucking women who torture themselves with a pair of empowering high heel shoes designed for fashion rather than function."

Maria surveyed Carmilla once again. The last time she had seen her, Carmilla was slightly haggard, with dark knotted hair. She was still hot but nowhere near this level. Her flesh no longer carried the burden of one suffering sleepless nights. Her demeanour was charged, aggressive and more confident than anyone she had ever seen. The deep red hair, her unblemished skin. Different from earlier, yes, but somehow the same. Something danced in Maria's mind, and as she tried to focus on this intrusion, she momentarily imagined Carmilla could read her thoughts. Maria chose not to enquire further…

"Of course, right away, I could see right through his shit, but I indulged in his game as I contemplated how it would come back to haunt him later. I acted like a giddy schoolgirl facing her crush to allow him to think he had the upper hand, but we all know men are only after one thing, and they will let nothing get in their way. Betrayal and lust are diseases which infest the soul, and I will no longer suffer the fools, and you shouldn't either!"

Carmilla spun around and began pacing slowly towards Maria. The light swarmed and stretched between them, and Maria started to feel nauseous and off balance.

"He took me back to his place, and I allowed him to touch me. I even followed him into the bedroom and allowed him to fuck me. I wanted him to recognise me before I punished him. You see, I had it all planned out. I wanted to see it in his eyes...to see me...that was until he told me about an old friend who owns a lodge. A friend that used to be his wingman back in the day. And that Dominic could get a discount and that he would take us there one day."

*An old friend from the past.*

"So I decided to wait until then to get them both together. But imagine my surprise to be invited along yesterday...by you no less... pretending to be him...so here I am..."

Maria commanded Carmilla's gaze, displaying no obvious reaction to her story. Behind the cogs of her eyes, her brain struggled to work with the coincidences from Carmilla's recollection. Only a few days ago, Maria's life was imperfect but normal...and she could have lived with that or willingly committed herself to the grave. How dare Carmilla, this reflection of all she wasn't, come in and turn everything upside down? A counterpart of all that made Maria jealous—of someone who wished to be left alone and did not appreciate those who desired her.

"The reason we are sat here now is fate, Maria. How else could all of the pieces be arranged this way? It's almost like a chess board, waiting for one of us to make the first move. To take the lead."

Maria tracked over these words and organised them into a workable string of events. Once again, the similarities between her experience and much of Carmilla's were uncanny. Indeed, there were too many coincidences: the trip to the cabin, the storm, the cancellations, Dominic and his friend, and Maria going through Dominic's phone…surely…

…was Carmilla real?

Was *she* real?

One thing was for sure—something they didn't share. While Carmilla was desperate to rid their lives of the monsters, Maria was now keen to indulge their company.

*Everyone fucking leaves me…*

Maria concluded at that moment that no one ever

would again.

Carmilla placed a clear vial between them on the table, allowing Maria to survey the liquid inside. Maria glanced at what looked to be a small aftershave bottle. She recalled finding a similar bottle—precisely the same—in Dominic's washbag. He had calmly told her it was just a small container to carry aftershave when travelling.

"It's amazing to think this unremarkable bottle could produce so much damage…"

Carmilla's statement hung in the air whilst Maria took the vial in her hand, unscrewing the lid as she spoke…

"…but isn't this just perfume …"

Maria held the vial under her nose, but its contents were without fragrance. Carmilla took back the bottle and held it beneath the light.

She stood up and walked to the patio window.

"…not perfume. Would a drop of perfume make you lose control of your faculties? To allow them to do what they did to me?"

An image of Dominic twisting and crawling towards Maria through the darkness. The sharpened heels of Carmilla's shoes disappearing into the barman's eyes. The sound of tissue snapping. A twitching body with no face…

*…who even am I anymore…?*

"Would a drop of perfume cause you and Dominic to pass out so heavily that I could inflict my vengance whilst you slept?"

Now confused, Maria couldn't make sense of the timeline.

"If it was you…how did you get here so fast?"

"Now come on, Maria. Really? I already knew you were both coming here. I was here before you arrived. How do you think I spiked that bottle of champagne? They leave these places open to the elements to save time when checking in. I have always been one step ahead of the game."

Maria felt a jolt of panic shuddering over her skin as she sunk into a recollection involving that same bottle which Dominic carried. The one she had never seen again after he must have hidden it from her.

Carmilla picked up the vial and smiled.

"Sometimes, fate requires a bit of a nudge!"

## CHAPTER FIFTEEN

Carmilla's words echoed in Maria's mind and were joined increasingly by the grumbling storm, which proceeded with a flash of lightning. It seemed odd to her that with the rising intensity of its wrath, she became more distant from reality, as though she was gazing through a lens at events that had already happened. Déjà vu once again consumed her, and she explored fruitlessly for various options to explain this unsettling sensation.

*Back in the hot tub earlier, she had considered ending things. Not to mention a few weeks ago when she considered jumping off the bridge after she argued with…Dom…Dominic…and then Carmilla had arrived.*

Maria questioned her existence, but something deep within her had already started to accept the only available solutions.

Maybe she was already dead, and this was her vivid afterlife. She had read once that your life can flash before you at death. Was the storm outside purely her perception of being underwater in the tub whilst death washed over her?

As she cast her gaze back to Carmilla, she wondered how long it would be until the trauma of all that had happened would finally catch up with her and allow her to rest, for the truth to unfold and set her free. The multiple coincidences stood out as impossible to accept without a highly irrational alignment of the stars.

The unrelenting wind battered trees, woodland, and buildings in its furious wake, starkly contrasting Maria's demeanour. Strangely, she couldn't even distinguish her heart rate, which fuelled the concept that she was no longer a living, breathing person but a mere spectator to a certainty she already knew. She remained calm.

Since the initial shock after finding Dominic, it occurred to her that she possibly had a hidden strength—a defensive response, allowing her to take things such as this in her stride. Almost as if the demise of Dominic had released her from a burden, and she had to admit, it felt good. It felt even better knowing that when she did close her eyes again, she would no longer be lonely. Dominic's brutally adulterated flesh would be there to welcome her. She pinched herself sharply, just to be sure. Although a surge of pain gave false promise that she was still coherent within the world, she understood that to be merely a memory or reflex carried over…something she would get used to.

Maria perceived the cabin walls to be stretching away as her psyche restructured, merging her prematurely accepted deductions with Carmilla's revelations. Her spirit tingled as a flood of images danced around her like pieces of a jigsaw puzzle, arranging themselves into their true and singular formation.

She could not be sure yet whatever part Carmilla played in all of this, but she knew she was heading towards the closure of this ordeal. Carmilla had just told her that she had monsters living in her fucking brain…Jesus Christ…and she still wasn't fucking content. Some people are just never happy.

*Whereas I would simply kill just for the company…*

Maria smiled as words she had never previously uttered sang in the atmosphere. A rising acceptance manifested inside of her. Carmilla's secrets hadn't satisfied her. She sought a more profound knowledge behind the whispers that stirred in the shadows, but all Carmilla wanted was to be rid of them.

Her mind blazed with the promise of the shuffling presence of Dominic as he wandered the coils of her subconscious in constant darkness. A grotesquely disfigured creature being horrifically tortured by unfathomable squirming entities, feeding on its suffering. A beast which used to be the man she loved…but the man she loved was nothing more than a rapist, so he deserved to be imprisoned. And Maria would be his governor. Whatever fluttered within her was now potent…intoxicating…she no longer cared if she was alive, dead or dreaming.

Carmilla had been talking, but Maria hadn't heard her entirely…about getting rid of the monsters so they could finally be together. But why would she want that? With Carmilla present, Maria no longer existed. If it weren't for her heightened senses, she would have sworn she was a ghost…

"...I did this for us, Maria...and for everyone else that those filthy cunts took advantage of. And once that rain eases off, we are going to burn this fucking place to the ground."

Maria finally yielded to the whispering certainty of her subsequent actions, which writhed and clutched onto the tendrils of her perception—the cacophony of a new existence...

Carmilla had materialised from the storm to save her. She always showed up when Maria needed her most...

The whisperings took shape as they danced and flourished, filling the gaps in Maria's fractured mind. Carmilla's spectre ate away at Maria's flesh like a plague...

...just as memories infested Carmilla as monsters, Maria may have fashioned Carmilla as her own tainted projection...

...Carmilla simply did not exist...

\*

Carmilla wasn't sure what kind of response to expect from Maria. Still, she had become astute at reading people over the years. The gaze that met her across the table was one of loneliness, of sincerity, and of someone she cared deeply for...

...but not just cared for...

Maria was her true love. A lost soul like her. Together, they could keep the monsters at bay. Oh, how she wished for the sweet mercy of silence, and when that day came, she would hide away from society and be at one with her thoughts and with Maria. Maybe they could forge a new life as they assisted one another in fighting off all the demons that afflicted them, like that fucking asshole Dominic.

Carmilla reached across the table, palms up. Maria smiled pensively and took her hands. She did harvest a notion of jealousy at how easily Maria blended in, about how she was never bombarded with attention and that she had never experienced the pain and physical debridement of rape. This stark contrast to Carmilla ate away at her. The heat from Maria's touch seemed to frolic and swirl inside her, electrifying her with a sensation she hadn't encountered before. This was a person she genuinely cared about. Fucking hell, she had now murdered two fucking assholes for both of their benefits. So the absolute least Maria could do was love her back.

Love… a word she had never uttered, a word she had shied away from forever. And now, opposite her, the girl she had previously broken ties with because she had gotten too close. Now, Carmilla began to feel weak but also protected…

"I…I…"

Carmilla struggled to finish her sentence. Maria, who now dominated the room, led Carmilla to her feet.

"I know you do, Carmilla…and I do too."

She lost herself in Maria's embrace and cried for the first time in recent memory. The pressure in the air encouraged their physical attributes to collide, to commence merging their unseen connection.

"It's nearly dawn, Carmilla. How are we going to deal with this mess?"

Carmilla laughed at this enquiry, "I told you, we will torch this place to the ground. Burn away all the evidence, and we can vanish. It will be so perfect…"

*…to shed my skin from all of this…*

"…the storm will eventually pass…and there is no one else in these cabins, apart from us, not until tomorrow afternoon anyway, according to the leger in reception."

Carmilla spoke with sincerity. To her, each of her victims deserved what she had done to them. Their choices were now firmly embedded in their flesh, exorcised from her subconscious. Now, she could finally face a future no longer condemned to the monsters that writhed and stirred in her psyche. Nature had imposed upon them the final storm of the season so that it and they could shed their skins.

"Carmilla, that sounds perfect. Hey, I have an idea. Shall we head outside and sit in the rain, just like we did the last time we were together?"

Carmilla now obeyed Maria and followed her onto the decking.

# CHAPTER SIXTEEN

Maria understood Carmilla to be no less than an unhinged reflection of herself—a confused apparition without the consequence of her actions. Nonetheless, she took Carmilla's hand in her own and led them both outside onto the decking as needles of rain reddened their skin.

Carmilla removed her clothing, and Maria gasped aloud at her beauty. She couldn't help but compare herself with her projected companion, who seemed to glisten and shine under the shimmer of rain which had finally begun to yield. As Carmilla stepped into the hot tub, her skin reddened further from the heat. Maria noticed how her *own* skin warmed simultaneously and felt a stirring of pleasure filling the coils of her abdomen. Maria's response did not feel strange; it was almost as though they were in synchronicity.

*Who the hell was she anymore?*

Maria's heart danced at the words that flashed before her as though on a cinema screen. She now knew exactly who she was, and this certainty satisfied many unanswered questions, such as why Carmilla's presence caused Maria to become invisible and why her thoughts and feelings manifested in Maria's mind, just as if they were the same person…

…Sure, there were slight physical differences, but that could be attributed to how they carried themselves—how the world perceived them. But the world had wronged them both…and the resilience of her fractured soul had conjured a tangibly different representation of herself.

Carmilla…*Scarlett.*

As the dying rain buzzed over the decking, she could no longer feel its teeth on her flesh. All she could feel was the vibrations from the tub, even though she was standing outside the tub watching Carmilla. Would their connection prompt the transformation needed to ascertain who Maria was? She had to act prior to the rain eroding her fading consciousness.

*Was Maria, indeed, Carmilla? Or was Carmilla actually*

*Maria...or were they both somehow Scarlett?*

Maria surrendered to the pending conviction of her fate. And did so as the sky grumbled in agreement, followed by a blinding light which split the horizon.

"Hey, Maria, are you not going to join me?"

The rain melted into the decking, and Maria was granted freedom from her physical restraints as nature momentarily took control of her impulses, allowing her more profound desires to flourish. She made peace with who she was. With the birth of a new day in a few hours and the storm's departure, nature itself whispered to her the promise that this was the start of her metamorphosis.

"I will be right there."

\*

Maria handed Carmilla a vodka and invited her to neck it before the rain diluted its contents. Carmilla swiftly backed it in one gulp as Maria joined her in the tub. The rain washed over their bodies, glistening and merging with the hot, soothing water. Almost an hour passed without a word between them as they shared the void of warmth whilst hidden eyes watched eagerly from somewhere nearby.

Feeling a sudden fatigue burrowing into her, Carmilla eased forward to switch the bubbles on the hot tub and leaned back against the side. She wondered if the monsters would leave her alone now that she had committed both men to the grave. If nothing had changed, what then? She wasn't quite ready to find out yet. First, she would enjoy the tranquillity before facing the stark reality of the new day, and she couldn't wait to burn this place to the ground.

It had been a long day, and with daylight shimmering against the slowing rain, a yawn worked its way across Carmilla's face. Her head became quite heavy.

"Another vodka?"

Maria was outside the tub now, and Carmilla lifted a trembling hand to take the glass from her. She felt numb at the temples, her senses anaesthetised against the elements. The glass fell from her grip as her eyes rolled back, and the water swallowed her...

*...Carmilla melted into the darkness as she surrendered to an unbearable compulsion for sleep, her faculties bound by silence*

*and inaction. Above the surface of the water, as she managed to break free for a moment, Maria leered at her. And so, too, did something else.*

*As she sunk helplessly into the bubbling abyss, they drew closer, manifesting, waiting for her. She screamed, but that only drew them closer. She tried to assert control to get away, but they were already on top of her. Dominic unnaturally twisted on all fours, the eyeless barman. As her life flashed before her, water filled her lungs, and two wretched creatures reached out to her…welcoming her into their vile embrace.*

*…she could hear the slowing of her heart as memories of the past crawled through her soul, intensifying as the light was forced out of her mind. With the sweet mercy of death upon her, she prayed to be free from this hell, once and for all, and the clutching monsters fell silent….*

*…Sleep well…my angel…*

## CHAPTER SEVENTEEN

The sun blazed down from an azure sky as the mist lifted from the hills. Moisture shimmered as a mirage under the sudden heat, which warmed away the cold yawn of the morning. Drenched fields and overflowing streams had seeped into the road, leaving the valleys waterlogged and undrivable to most.

The distant ringing of a police siren approached from the motorway, grinding swiftly along the single road to Lakeside Cabins, splashing over the regular scatterings of congealed rain that had pooled into the pits and hollows.

Police Sergeant Damien Peters rolled the window down and adjusted his collar as he navigated the road. His radio earlier picked up a call to check on Lakeside Cabins as the owner—a tall, peaked man called Bob

Warner—struggled to contact reception. Bob was concerned that the storm had potentially destroyed his beloved campsite. Unable to reach the place until next week, he asked his old friend Damo to drop by to see how things were.

Damo had lived in the area all his life. He knew each rolling green hill by name, having spent much of his childhood in the wilderness. Any chance for a paid day of solitude from civilisation was perfect for him. His job was primarily relaxed, with scarcely any crime to tend to, which meant minimal paperwork and more time cruising on the road in his Land Rover.

He often popped into Lakeside Cabins for a coffee and to show his face. Even more so now since the owner had employed that fuckwit, Justin. He didn't like that guy. Something about him was off. Bob had informed Damo that some people are just different and that Justin was a good worker who didn't make any trouble.

The wheels bounced into a pothole, and water splashed up the side of the truck, causing Damo to curse and ease off the accelerator. Damo didn't expect any problem at the cabin besides the likely power cut, so there was no inherent rush. If so, he would remain in situ until the emergency power team arrived to fix it.

Damo smiled at this—just another day in the call of duty. He manoeuvred the truck up the hill through the trees and could see the lodges at the summit. He would check in the bar first, then scope out the remainder of the area. He couldn't see any tracks indicating that cars had entered the place recently.

Damo steered the truck into the space outside reception, killed the engine and siren, but left the flashing lights on so that anyone nearby could at least see him. The car park was empty, but he would check the cabins next to see if there were any guests.

He listened intently for any signs of movement or anyone calling for help. Once satisfied that the area was clear, he approached the main door and knocked it loudly before trying to push it open. The door was locked, and Damo couldn't make out much more than a vacant bar through the small window beside the entrance.

He banged on the door again.

"Hello. Police… Is anyone home?"

After waiting a few moments for a response, he

made his way around the cabin's perimeter, checking all the apertures to see what he could find.

The glass panes were slightly misted inside, likely from the coal fire and lack of ventilation, but one looked to have a drawing in the mist—like a crossed-out loveheart. Damo had to pull himself up to glimpse inside, and what he saw caused him to drop quickly to the floor and stagger back to his vehicle to call in reinforcements.

*

Within an hour, Lakeside Cabins was cordoned off. A small team forced their way into the bar to find the deformed corpse of Justin Tailor, who it later turned out was a convicted sex offender and had incredibly managed to avoid being detected by not just the owner of the cabins, but by the incompetent local police sergeant Damien Peters.

Next, and once the immediate area was clear, crime scene investigators began photographing the interior, including Justin, the broken bottle which had been used as a weapon, and the peculiar loveheart glazed on the window.

Armed officers then systematically entered the cabins, surrounding each side before the point man gained entry with his pistol steady.

Their efforts to find evidence of what had happened to Justin proved fruitless until they reached the last cabin. The team moved over the decking area to the patio doors, as they had done on the other cabins, but this door, in particular, was ajar, which alerted them to treat this cabin with more trepidation.

After clearing the perimeter, the team finally made their way into the master bedroom to find the brutally defiled carcass of a man later identified as Dominic White, who investigators learned was an acquaintance of Justin the barman. Additionally, they uncovered a recording device concealed behind a painting on the wall overlooking the bed. They also found a water-damaged mobile phone. Both were sent off to forensics for analysis.

With two dead bodies, they spent a few hours surveying the vicinity, as it was now clear they were potentially dealing with a double murder. The lodges were turned inside out, and the team searched under the decking and even in the hot tubs before cordoning them off with blue tape.

Upon lifting the lid of the last hot tub, they revealed the drowned body of a young woman with bright red hair, probably in her late twenties. On the table beside her rested a single glass.

*

The police investigation took several weeks to clear up, drawing the attention of many local news channels. Newsreaders around the country spoke about how three bodies had been discovered at Lakeside Cabins and that one of these was sex offender Justin Tailor, who had somehow managed to gain employment at the lodge.

During subsequent examinations, the police scrutinised the inferior quality visual footage on the camera, which had been set up to record the period between ten p.m. and two a.m. on the evening Dominic arrived at the cabin. The clip showed a girl, identified only as Scarlett from text messages on her phone, performing a sexual act on Dominic before brutally murdering him. Scarlett then went on to murder Dominic's friend, Justin, in the bar before drowning herself in the tub after ingesting the contents of a vial located in the lodge.

From Justin's laptop, the investigating team reviewed video footage of many lodge visitors engaging in private moments of intimacy and young girls drying themselves off after a shower. Emails on the laptop sent to Dominic from Justin contained attachments of videos involving Dominic and more than ten unknown girls.

With enough evidence assembled, both murders were eventually pinned on Scarlett, who, according to the text messages, was invited to the lodge by Dominic, the only named on-site guest in the reception booking ledger.

Scarlett is yet to be formally identified.

# CHAPTER EIGHTEEN

*Dominic screamed in anguish, his sightless head flopping back and forth like a pendulum, as hordes of ravenous creatures with unrelenting urges for his cavernous wounds pleasured themselves like a frantic gathering of maggot-covered faceless parasites.*

*Maria enjoyed witnessing them slide and frolic amongst the blackness. They slithered and writhed their pulsating bodies of mass, like overfed worms, leaking a thick fluid from openings in the crests of their awful formations.*

*She stood untouched and yet unnoticed by the horrifying sexually charged pandemonium, gleefully observing the wretched torso of Dominic shuddering in endless agony as the countless monsters took turns on him. His brutally contorted limbs were unable to drag him away from their vile clutches.*

*Dominic…her pet…*

*Once satisfied, the monsters would disappear into the shadows, where she could hear them squelching and devouring something, then regrouping to pleasure themselves over Dominic; a pitiful plaything to serve them for eternity.*

*Further behind Dominic, another eyeless organism wept as the hordes burrowed their way inside of him, saturating the contours of his flesh with their wriggling and festering hunger before their fattened formations burst free from the gaping wounds which used to offer him sight.*

*Maria watched as they defiled these two souls, knowing that each time she returned, they would be regenerated to suffer their humiliating tortures. When she visited them, she was intoxicated by their company, and she knew they could hear the excitement dancing in her.*

*Maria was often compelled to call out to them to offer them a false beacon of hope for their suffering. She loved it when they struggled towards her on weak appendages, weighed down by these sexually motivated demons, hunting for her.*

*Her pets had no purpose but to wander within the coils of her mind. Both blind and helpless, they had eternity to work out the patterns and fissures of her Labyrinth. They would eventually learn about her fears. And with little else to do but understand those fears, they would help one another…. Together, maybe they would find her…*

*Her dreams always unfolded in response to the image of*

*Carmilla materialising at the conclusion. Her beautiful form was forever drawn towards Maria's escalating excitement as she appeared behind the trembling manifestations of her creation, trapped alongside these creatures who joined her when the darkness feasted. As always, Carmilla's apparition fed on Maria's. Even in the absence of light, she cast Maria into the abyss once more…unseen, as the accursed beings of Dominic and Justin now retreated…*

*It was as if Maria's inherent fear of losing those closest to her was feeding on the abstract reality she had fashioned, causing the foundations of her world to collapse. Maria wondered how long she could keep them contained before they left her.*

*…everyone leaves me in the end…*

# FINAL CHAPTER

The bar's ambience on a Friday night was less lively than what she was used to, but it allowed her to be seen. To be admired. And she was getting much better at her *fishing*, as she liked to call it. Empowered and unfaltering, she had never felt so alive. She could see her target approaching from her peripherals, and although a warm glow filled her being, she allowed it not to show in her demeanour.

"Excuse me. Is it okay if I join you?"

She motioned, without facing him, to sit across the table. After surveying the bar, he obeyed. His friends jostled and gestured towards the table as they awaited the outcome of the exchange. Finally, she turned, showing him her best smile while crossing her slender leg towards him.

He was handsome and full of confidence. His

grey three-piece suit complemented his physique, giving width to his shoulders and tapering in neatly at the waist. His face creased perfectly at all the right angles, and a neat dashing of stubble added a subtle ruggedness to his clean-cut appearance. His hair was magnificently thick, and he obviously spent much time on himself to stand out from the crowd, his charisma oozing like invisible maggots crawling and squirming in the space between them.

He was no match for her, though, and she beckoned him closer, with eyes large and lustrous, popping from a pale complexion bordered by exquisite and delicate flowing hair. She had mastered the secret act of seduction, and he would be her next conquest.

It mattered to her that he was desirable, but his toned physique was a bonus. She would enjoy every inch of him prior to the inevitable sacrifice of his flesh. How long he would last before she fed him to the shadows, she did not yet know. Like everyone else in her life, he would eventually wrong her. But one covenant kept her warm…

*…he would never leave her…*

If he ever tried to free himself from his new

existence, from her, she would absorb his soul. And within the darkness of her dreams, he would have company, but more importantly, so would she. Any previously ingrained fear of being alone was now cast into a bottomless void by the magnitude of her…collection.

With each sacrificial lamb, she would accumulate more strength, and she had become quite an expert at the game. It was easy to blend in until it was time to stand out. The nuances of attraction offered many tools for her to fashion each interaction to her will.

From somewhere in the labyrinth of her mind, she could sense them squirming in anticipation of the new arrival. They always became excited near feeding, which only served to whet her appetite.

She licked her lips as she gazed at him, fully tuned in to the situation and keen to indulge in her charade.

*Green light!*

His smooth, gravel voice sent electricity rushing through every fissure of her body.

"What's your name?"

She allowed a smirk to manifest as she flirtatiously flicked her long, flowing, dyed red hair behind her ear.

"Scarlett."

THE END

# ABOUT THE AUTHOR

Daniel Lorn is a horror author from the United Kingdom.

With his spine-chilling debut, Obsession, in 2022, Daniel marked his entry into the realm of horror literature. The resounding acclaim for his unique brand of horror quickly fuelled his creative drive, leading to the release of PACT, See You Later, RED, & more recently, Sins of the Wronged.

Daniel's writing style has been lauded for its ability to transform the ordinary into the monstrous. While he has primarily delved into psychological horror with Obsession, PACT, and RED, his true passion lies in the world of supernatural horror, as seen in See You Later. This genre will be the primary focus of his future works, & Daniel promises many more spine-tingling tales to come.

Author Website: www.daniellornhorror.co.uk

# OTHER BOOKS BY THE AUTHOR

### **OBSESSION**

*"HAUNTING & BEAUTIFULLY WRITTEN"*

*"TRULY DISTURBING"*

*"A PSYCHOLOGICAL MAZE THAT HAS LOST ITS OWN EXIT"*

*"BEAUTIFULLY TWISTED"*

It had never occurred to me that so many forbidden and unimaginable desires lurked beyond the veil of existence. For years, I had suffered in ignorance of this revelation, allowing my forgotten appetites to rot away within the depths of my blood. Although blind within the darkness, these cravings desperately longed to be observed. But now they stirred. Now they danced gracefully on the surface of my sanity, having floated up from depths unexplored.

## **PACT**

*"TERRIFYINGLY EXCELLENT"*

*"DELICIOUSLY GOOD"*

*"SPINE TINGLINGLY FRIGHTENING"*

*"DARK, HAUNTING & HEARTBREAKING"*

*"LORN IS A WORDSMITH"*

Can you ever really know someone?

With his wife recently deceased, William has fallen into a spiral of depression and alcoholism. Memories haunt him when he is sober. Memories he struggles to contain, no matter how hard he tries. But there is something else that comes with those memories. Something which causes him to question his sanity. Something unwelcome and deeply terrifying.

## **SEE YOU LATER**

*"ABSOLUTELY TERRIFYING"*

*"HAUNTING & MASTERFULLY WRITTEN"*

*"MESMERISING"*

*"UNSETTLING & IMPACTFUL"*

*"THE STUFF OF NIGHTMARES"*

Beyond the shadows of physical comprehension is a world we only touch the boundaries of during our most terrifying nightmares. Whether our imaginations fashion the monsters that lurk there or whether the dead themselves walk these realms is unknown to most.

Some of us are cursed with the ability to peel back the fabric of reality to glimpse at this inconceivable domain.

Others are destined to walk there, amongst the damned.

## **RED**

*"PSYCHOLOGICAL HORROR AT ITS FINEST"*

*"TRULY MIND-BLOWING"*

*"A REMARKABLE UNCOMFORTABLE READ"*

*"GENUINELY FRIGHTENING"*

*"ABSOLUTELY SAVAGE"*

When recent events threaten to tear his world apart, a broken soul is drawn to a whisper manifesting within the darkness.

A whisper that offers him the faith to face the shadows of his past and the ability to deal with those who have wronged him.

Printed in Great Britain
by Amazon